SLOWLY, GRADUALLY THE GREAT ROCK BEGAN TO MOVE.

Hunting for Hidden Gold

HARDY BOYS MYSTERY STORIES

HUNTING FOR HIDDEN GOLD

By

FRANKLIN W. DIXON

NEW YORK
GROSSET & DUNLAP
PUBLISHERS

CONTENTS

CHAPTER I

IN THE STORM

"A FORTUNE in hidden gold! That certainly sounds mighty interesting."

Frank Hardy folded up the letter he had just been reading aloud to his brother.

"Dad has all the luck," replied Joe. "I'd give anything to be working with him on a case like that."

"Me, too. This case is a bit out of the ordinary."

"Where was the letter postmarked?"

"Somewhere in Montana. A gold-mining camp called Lucky Bottom."

"Montana! Gee, but I wish he could have taken us with him. We've never been more than two hundred miles from home."

"And I've never seen a mine in my life, much less a real mining camp."

The Hardy boys looked at one another re-

gretfully. They had just received a letter
from their father, Fenton Hardy, an internationally famous detective, who had been called
West but a fortnight previous on a mysterious
mission. The letter gave the boys their first
inkling of the nature of the case that had sum
moned their father from Bayport, on the At
lantic coast, to the mining country of Montana

"A fortune in hidden gold," repeated
Frank. "I hope he finds it all right."

"It was stolen from one of the big com-
panies, wasn't it?"

"Yes. He says that an entire shipment of
bullion was stolen before it left the camp, so
they believe it must have been hidden somewhere in the neighborhood."

"And his job is to find it."

"If he can. And the thieves as well."

Joe sighed. "I sure would like to be out
there right now. We might be able to help
him."

"Well, we've helped him in other cases, but
I guess we're out of luck this time. Montana
is too far away."

"Yes, and we have to keep on going to
school. I'll be glad when we're through school
and can be regular detectives like dad."

Frank grinned. "No use grouching about
it," he said cheerfully. "Our time will come
some day."

"Yes, but it seems a long time coming," replied Joe, smiling ruefully.

"Oh, in a few more years we'll be going all over the country just like dad, solving robberies and murders and having all sorts of excitement. We haven't done too badly so far, anyway."

"Yes, we had the fun of discovering the tower treasure."

"And running down the counterfeiters."

"Yes; and solving the mystery of the house on the cliff and finding out about Blacksnake Island."

The boys were referring to previous cases in which they had been involved and in which their ability had been proved. But it had been several months since any adventure or excitement had come their way and they were feeling restless, the more so now that they knew their father was at that moment in the remote mining camp in the West engaged on a mystery that seized their imagination.

"Hidden gold!" said Joe, half to himself. "That *would* be a case worth working on."

"Forget it," laughed his brother. "There's no use making yourself miserable wishing we were out there, because we're not and it doesn't look as if there's much chance that we shall be. Perhaps his old case isn't so exciting, anyway. You're not going to spend all

Saturday wishing for something you can't have. Don't forget we're to go out with Chet and Jerry this afternoon."

"That's right," declared Joe. "I'd almost forgotten. We were to go skating, weren't we?"

"Yes; and it's about time we started or the others will be going without us."

This possibility moved Joe to action and in a few moments the Hardy boys had dismissed their father's letter from their minds and were rummaging in a cupboard beneath the stairs for their skates. They had planned to meet their chums at the mouth of Willow River, a stream that ran from the mountains down through the farm lands to Barmet Bay, on which Bayport was located. It was a brisk, clear winter afternoon, ideal for an outing, and their Saturday holiday from Bayport high school was much too precious to be spent indoors.

Their Aunt Gertrude, an elderly, crotchety maiden lady of certain temper and uncertain years, eyed them suspiciously as they came into the hallway wtih their skates and began donning sweaters and warm gloves.

"Skating, hey?" she sniffed. "You'll go through the ice, I'll be bound."

The boys knew from experience that it was always best to placate Aunt Gertrude.

"We'll try not to, Aunt Gertrude," Frank assured her.

"You'll try not to! A lot of good that will do. If the ice isn't strong, all the trying in the world won't keep you from going through it. And the ice *isn't* strong. I'm sure it isn't. It can't be."

"The fellows have been skating on Willow River for more than a week now."

"Maybe so. Maybe so. They've been lucky, that's all I can say. You mark my words, that ice will break one of these fine days. I only hope you boys aren't on it when it does."

"I hope so too," laughed Frank, drawing on his gloves.

"It's no laughing matter," persisted Aunt Gertrude gloomily. "Well, I suppose if you will court death and destruction, an old lady like me can't do anything to stop you. Although you'd be better off at home studying. Run along. Run along."

"Good-bye, Aunt Gertrude."

"Run along. Be home early. Don't skate too far out. Don't get lost. Don't get caught in a snowstorm. I'm sure there's one coming up. I know the signs. My lumbago is troubling me again to-day. Don't forget to come back in time for tea."

Aunt Gertrude's favorite word was "don't" and she persisted in treating her nephews as though they were but a grade advanced from kindergarten. Mrs. Hardy was out for the afternoon and in her absence the worthy spinster rejoiced in her opportunity to exercise her authority. When she had exhausted her store of admonitions, the boys departed, and she watched them from the door with gloomy forebodings as to the ultimate outcome of their skating trip. Aunt Gertrude was a pessimist of the first water.

When the Hardy boys reached the foot of the street they found Chet Morton, rotund and jovial, and Jerry Gilroy, tall and red-cheeked, awaiting them.

"Just going to start without you," declared Chet, swinging his skates.

"We had a letter from dad and we were so interested in reading it that we mighty near forgot about the trip," confessed Frank.

"Where is he?"

"Out in Montana, in a mining camp, working on a case."

"Gosh, he's lucky!" said Jerry enviously.

"I'll say he is," agreed Frank. "Joe and I have just been wishing we could be out there with him."

"Well, we can't have everything," Chet said cheerfully. "Come on—I'll race you to Willow River."

He dashed off down the snow-covered street,

the others in close pursuit. The race was of short duration, for Willow River was some distance away, and the boys soon slowed down to a walk. At a more reasonable gait they continued their journey, and within half an hour had reached the river, now covered with a gleaming sheet of ice. In a few minutes the lads had donned their skates and were skimming off over the smooth surface.

The banks of the river were covered with snow and the trees along the shore were bare and black. Above the hills the sky was of a slaty gray.

"Looks like snow," Frank commented, as they skated on up the river.

"Oh, it'll blow over," answered Chet carelessly. "Let's go on up to Shallow Lake."

"We don't want to be away too long. It'll be dark before we get back."

"We can skate up there and back in a couple of hours. Come on."

It was a brisk, cold afternoon and the boys did not need much urging. Shallow Lake was back in the hills, but the boys made such good time over the glassy surface of the river that it was not long before they left the farm lands behind.

Frank Hardy cast an anxious glance at the sky every little while. He knew the signs of brooding storm and the peculiar haziness above the horizon indicated an approaching snowstorm. However, he said nothing, in the hope that they would be able to reach the mouth of the river again before the storm broke.

It was four o'clock before the Hardy boys and their chums reached Shallow Lake. It was a picturesque little body of water and the ice shone with a blue glare, smooth as glass and free of snow. It was a natural skating rink, and Chet Morton gave a whoop of delight as he went skimming out upon it.

The boys enjoyed skating on the lake so greatly that they scarcely noticed the first few flakes of snow that drifted down from the slaty sky, and it was not until the snowfall became so heavy that it almost blotted out the opposite hillsides that they thought of going back.

"Looks as if it's settling down for the night," Joe remarked. "We'd better start back before we get lost."

"Might as well," agreed Chet Morton, with a sigh. "I wish we'd come out here this morning. I'd like to skate here all day."

With Frank Hardy in the lead, the boys began to make their way toward Willow River, where it left the lake. They were about half a mile out on the open expanse of ice and the snow was now falling heavily. At first the

soft white flakes had merely drifted down.
Now they came scudding across the ice,
whipped by a rising wind.

"It'll be harder getting back," Frank said.
"The wind is against us."

The wind was indeed against them and it
was rising in volume. It came in quick, vio-
lent gusts, storming sheets of snow down upon
them, snow that stung their faces and erased
the scene before them in a white cloud. Then
it blew steadily, with increasing force. The
storm moaned and whistled about them. They
could scarcely see one another, save as dark,
shadowy figures skating steadily on toward the
gloomy line of hills that rose from the haze of
storm.

"Why, this is a regular blizzard!" Chet
Morton shouted.

As though in emphasis, the wind shrieked
down upon them with redoubled fury. The
snow was swirling across the flat surface of the
lake in great white sheets. The cold became
more intense. It became apparent that in a
few minutes even the near-by shores would be
blotted from view.

"Let's make for the shore!" called out
Frank. "We'll wait until it blows over."

There was a high cliff not far away, and
Frank judged that it would provide shelter
from the brunt of the storm until they should

be able to continue their journey. Clearly, it was inadvisable to go on, for the wind was against them and they were making little headway. Also, in the fury of the sweeping snow, it was possible that they might become separated. So they turned toward the cliff, that they could see dimly through the gray gloom.

The wind shrieked. The snow beat against them. The sharp flakes stung their faces, swept into their eyes. The hurricane seemed like a mighty wall, forcing them back. Doggedly, they skated on, into the face of the blizzard that seemed to be sapping their strength.

Chet Morton already was lagging behind. The snow was collecting on the ice in little heaps and banks that clogged their skates and made progress even more difficult.

The face of the cliff seemed a long distance away. And, with redoubled fury, the wind came howling down over the hills.

Frank was almost exhausted by the constant battle against the wind and snow, and he knew that the others, too, were tiring quickly. It would be death for them if they faltered now. They must reach the shelter of the cliff!

CHAPTER II

A Call for Help

Doggedly, the boys fought their way on through the blizzard.

Once Joe Hardy stumbled and fell prone in the snow. He was up again in a moment, but the incident testified to the difficulty of their progress. The cliff seemed no nearer. To add to their peril twilight was gathering and the gloom of the blizzard was intensified.

"We've *got* to make it," Frank muttered, gritting his teeth.

The boys were strung out in single file, Chet Morton in the rear. All were tiring. Frank skated more slowly to give the others an opportunity of catching up. When they were together again he waved his arm toward the gray mass that loomed through the storm ahead.

"Almost there!"

His words gave all of them new courage, and they redoubled their efforts. In a short while the force of the wind seemed to be decreasing They were now gaining the shelter of the cliff.

The snow had not collected so heavily on the surface of the ice, and they made better progress. In a few minutes they had skated into an area of comparative calm. They could still hear the screaming of the wind, and when they looked back the entire lake was an inferno of swirling snow, but in the shelter of the steep rocks they were protected from the full fury of the blizzard.

"Some storm!" grunted Chet, as he skated slowly to the base of the cliff and sat down on a frost-encrusted boulder.

"I'll say it is," agreed Jerry Gilroy, following Chet's example.

The Hardy boys leaned against the rocks. They were safe enough in this shelter unless the wind changed completely about, which was unlikely. With the approach of darkness it was growing colder, but all the boys were warmly clad and they had few fears on that score. Their chief worry was lest the storm should not die down in time to permit of their return to Bayport that night, because they knew their people would be worrying about them.

"I see where mother won't let *me* go skating again," declared Chet. "She's always afraid I'll get drowned or lost or something, and now she'll get such a scare that I'll never get out again."

"Aunt Gertrude will crow over this for a month," Joe put in. "She said before we started that we'd be sure to get into some kind of a mess."

"Well, we'll just have to wait here until the storm blows over, that's all," said Frank philosophically. "Even if it does get dark we can follow the river all right and get home easily enough. Perhaps the storm won't last very long."

The boys settled themselves down to wait in the lee of the high black rocks until the fury of the blizzard should have diminished. There seemed to be no indication that the storm was dying down and they resigned themselves to a wait of at least an hour. Frank scouted around in search of firewood, planning to light a blaze, but any wood there may have been along the shore had long since been snowed under and he had to give up the attempt.

While the boys are thus marooned by the storm in the shelter of the cliff it might be best to introduce them to new readers of this series.

Frank and Joe Hardy, sixteen and fifteen years old respectively, were the sons of Fenton Hardy, an internationally famous private detective, living in Bayport, on the Atlantic Coast. Although still in high school, both boys had inherited many of their father's deductive tendencies and his ability in his chosen profession and it was their ambition to some day become detectives themselves.

Their father had made an enviable name for himself. For many years he was with the New York Police Department, but had resigned to accept cases on his own account. He was known as one of the most astute detectives in the country and had solved many mysteries that had baffled city police and detective forces.

In the first volume of this series, "The Hardy Boys: The Tower Treasure," Frank and Joe Hardy solved their first mystery, tracing down a mysterious theft of jewels and bonds from a mansion on the outskirts of Bayport after their father had been called in on the case and had been forced to admit himself checkmated. The boys had received a substantial reward for their efforts and had convinced their parents that they had marked abilities in the work they desired to follow.

The second volume, "The Hardy Boys: The House on the Cliff," recounted the adventures of the boys in running down a criminal gang operating in Barmet Bay, and in the third volume, "The Hardy Boys: The Secret of the Old Mill," they aided their father materially in rounding up another gang.

The volume just previous to the present volume, "The Hardy Boys: The Missing Chums," told how they sought their chums,

Chet Morton and Biff Hooper, who had been kidnapped by a gang of crooks and taken to a sinister island off the coast.

As the boys waited in the shelter of the rocks they talked of some of the adventures they had undergone.

"This is the first bit of excitement we've had since we left Blacksnake Island," declared Chet. "I thought we were never going to have any adventures again."

"This isn't much of an adventure," Frank said, smiling, "but perhaps it's better than nothing. Although I must say it's a mighty cold and uncomfortable one," he added. "I wonder if we'll ever have any adventures like the ones we've gone through already."

"I think you've had your fill," grumbled Jerry Gilroy. "You've had more excitement than any other two fellows in Bayport."

"I suppose we have. Like the time the smugglers caught dad and kept him in the cave in the cliff and then caught us when we went to rescue him."

"And the time we got into the old mill and found the gang at work," added Joe.

"Or the fight on Blacksnake Island when you came after Biff Hooper and me," Chet Morton put in. "You've had enough adventure to last you a lifetime. What are you kicking about?"

"I'm not kicking. Just wondering if we'll ever have anything else happen to us."

"If this blizzard keeps up all night you can chalk down another adventure in your little red book," declared Jerry. "That is, if we don't freeze to death."

"Cheerful!"

"It doesn't look as if the wind is dying down, anyway."

They looked out into the swirling screen of snow. The wind, instead of diminishing, seemed to be increasing in fury and the snow was even sweeping in little gusts and eddies into their refuge at the base of the rocks. The swirling snow hid the opposite shore of the lake completely and the howling of the wind was rising in volume.

Suddenly they heard a strange crashing noise that came from directly overhead.

All looked up, startled.

"What was that?" asked Chet.

The crashing noise continued for a moment or so, then died away, drowned out by the roar of the wind and the sweep of the snow.

"Perhaps it was a tree blown over," suggested Jerry.

"A tree wouldn't make that much noise," Frank objected. For the crash had been unusually loud and prolonged and it had seemed to be accompanied by the snapping of timbers.

The boys waited, listening, but the sound had died away.

"It was right above us," Joe said.

Hardly had he spoken the words than there came a second crash, louder than the first, and then, with a rush and a roar, a great avalanche of snow came hurtling down upon the boys from the side of the cliff. The snow engulfed them, swept over them, almost buried them as they struggled to avoid it. Then, in all the uproar, they heard another thundering crash close at hand.

Spluttering and struggling to extricate themselves from the avalanche of snow that had swept down from above, the boys could scarcely realize what had happened. As for the origin of the crashing sound they had heard, it was still a mystery.

Then, above the clamor of the gale that seemed to rage in redoubled volume, they heard a faint cry. It came from the fog of swirling snow close by. Then the shrieking wind drowned the sound out, but the boys knew that it had been a cry for help.

Frank struggled free and lent Joe a helping hand until they were both clear of the great heap of snow and ice. Chet Morton and Jerry Gilroy also fought their way clear without difficulty, for the snow was soft and the avalanche had not been of great proportions.

"I heard some one call," Frank shouted. "Listen."

Shivering with cold, the boys stood knee-deep in snow and listened intently.

There came a lull in the gale.

Then, faintly, they heard the shout again.

"Help!" came the cry. "Help! Help!"

It came from somewhere immediately before them, and as the wind shifted just then Frank caught sight of a dark object against the surface of the snow.

"Come on!" he shouted to the others, and began plunging through the snow over to the object he had spied.

The boys reached it in a few minutes. To their unbounded astonishment they found that they were confronted by the side of a small cottage

CHAPTER III

JADBURY WILSON

In amazement, the Hardy boys and their chums stared at the cottage that had so strangely appeared in the snow.

"How did that get here?" shouted Chet Morton.

Frank waved his hand toward the top of the cliff.

"There was a little cottage up there," he told them. "It must have been blown off by the wind."

This, indeed, had been the case. Sheltered by the cliff, the boys had no adequate realization of the immense force of the hurricane. The little cottage at the top of the cliff had received the full brunt of the wind and had finally succumbed to the gale and to the force of a sudden avalanche of snow from farther up on the hillside. It had no foundation, and it had been swept away bodily.

The boys fought their way through the deep snow and inspected the little house. It had come through the terrific ordeal with surprisingly small damage. One side had crumpled under the force of the impact and the building was canted over at a precarious angle. But the roof and the other three sides were unbroken, thanks to the soft snow which had lessened the shock of the fall.

"There must be some one inside," Joe said. "Some one was shouting for help."

Frank found the door of the cottage and tried to open it, but it was jammed, as the house was not standing upright. Then he discovered a window, the glass of which was shattered, and with assistance from the others he made his way inside.

The interior of the place was wrecked. In the dim light Frank could see the broken boards and shattered timbers, the broken glass, the upturned stove, the smashed furniture— but there was no sign of any human being.

"Doesn't seem to be any one here," he called out to the others.

Just then he heard a sigh. It came from beneath an upturned cot at one side of the room. He investigated and saw a hand emerging from beneath the cot. In a few minutes he had raised the small bed and found an old man lying face downward on the floor.

"Help me out!" muttered the old man feebly.

Frank called to the others, and one by one they came scrambling through the window. Together, they raised the old man to his feet and set him down on the cot, which they turned to an upright position again. Painfully, the old fellow rubbed his aching joints.

"No bones broken," he said, at last. "I'm lucky I wasn't killed."

"You might have been crushed to death," Frank interposed.

"It's lucky you boys were near," he said. "I'd have frozen to death if I'd been left pinned under that cot. I mightn't have been found for days. But it takes a lot to kill Jadbury Wilson. I guess my time ain't come yet."

The old man looked around and smiled feebly at the lads. He was small but sturdy of frame, with kindly blue eyes and a gray beard.

"I've often thought it was dangerous to live in a place at the top of a cliff like that," he said. "There've been times when the wind was so strong I was afraid it would pick up my house and lift it clean out into the lake. But, somehow, it always stood up until to-day. It all came so suddenly I hardly knew what was happenin'. Mighty good thing the house landed right side up. How did you lads come to be near by?"

"We were on a skating trip and we got caught in the storm," Frank told him. "We took refuge at the foot of the cliff and we were standing there when we heard the crash. Then we heard some one call.''

''That was me. I didn't think there was any use of hollerin', but I hollered just the same, although I didn't think there was a human soul within three miles.''

Jadbury Wilson got up off the cot, but subsided back with a groan of pain.

''I got banged and bumped around too much,'' he said. ''Thought I'd get busy and try to straighten things up around here.''

''We'll do that,'' said Jerry Gilroy promptly.

''Everythin's pretty well smashed up,'' observed the old man. ''But you could mebbe fix up the stove so it would work again. Looks as if we're all here to stay until the storm blows over.''

The boys made Jadbury Wilson comfortable on his cot and then they set to work to restore some semblance of order to the interior of the little cabin. They managed to patch up openings in the walls through which the snow was drifting, and although one side of the cottage had collapsed completely there was still sufficient room in which to move about. They nailed a tarpaulin over the broken window, righted the table and chairs and picked up the tin dishes that were scattered about on the floor. The stove gave them most trouble, but they were able to set the stovepipe up again and light a fire so that before long a comfortable warmth began to pervade the interior of their shelter.

Jadbury Wilson, lying on the cot, approved of their efforts.

"We're in out of the storm, anyway," he said. "That's the main thing. And from the sound of that wind, it ain't as yet dyin' down any."

Frank Hardy drew aside the tarpaulin and looked out. It was dark now, and with nightfall the blizzard seemed to have increased in volume. The wind beat against the sides of the cabin, the snow swished madly against the roof.

"We're marooned here for the night," he told his chums.

"It could be worse," remarked Joe. "We're lucky to be under cover."

"I'll say we are," declared Chet. "Might as well make the best of it."

"How about eating?" demanded Jerry.

"You'll find tea and bread and bacon in the cupboard," said Jadbury Wilson. "I'm feelin' sort of hungry myself."

The boys rummaged about in the cupboard, which was undamaged, and found provisions. The water had been spilled, but Frank melted some snow on the stove and after a while had the kettle boiling. The fragrant smell of frying bacon pervaded the cabin and in due time supper was served, all doing full justice to the meal. Afterward, they washed the dishes and set about making themselves comfortable for the night.

Jadbury Wilson possessed but the one narrow cot, so the boys saw they would be obliged to sleep on the floor of the cabin. However, the old man had plenty of blankets, and it was decided to have each lad stand watch for two hours in order to keep the fire going. In spite of the fact that the bitter wind swept through chinks and crannies in the cabin walls, the place was comfortably warm, the fire radiating a good heat in the confined space.

Jadbury Wilson was disconsolate.

"Troubles never seem to come one at a time," he groaned, lying on the cot. "This is the finishin' touch."

"Have you been having bad luck, Mr. Wilson?" asked Frank, sympathetically.

"I've had nothin' but bad luck for more'n a year past now. This is the worst blow yet. I'll never be able to put this house back on the cliff again."

"Oh, perhaps it isn't as bad as that," said Joe cheerfully. "You might have been badly hurt. There's that to be thankful for."

"I suppose you're right, lad. I suppose you're right. I ought to be glad I'm still alive. But when you're gettin' old and poor and you ain't able to work like you've been used to and everythin' seems to be goin' against you, it ain't so easy to keep cheerful."

The old man seemed so down-hearted that the boys did their best to console him, but this final disaster to his humble cottage had proved a hard blow. He lacked the resiliency and optimism of youth.

"There was a time when I should have been worth lots of money," he told the boys. "And if I had my rights I ought to be worth lots of money to-day. But here I am, with not many years ahead of me, livin' away out here alone in a little two-by-twice cabin, and now the wind has to come along and blow it into the lake. It don't seem fair, somehow."

"What do you do for a living, Mr. Wilson?" asked Chet Morton.

"I've been doin' a bit of trappin' and hunt-in' lately," the old man replied. "Most of my life I've been a miner. I've traveled all over the country."

The boys were at once interested.

"A miner, were you?"

"Yep. I've been in Montana and Nevada in the early days."

At mention of Montana the Hardy boys

glanced at one another. Jadbury Wilson did not seem to notice.

"I've been in the Klondike in the rush of ninety-eight and I've been up in Cobalt and the Porcupine, too. Made a little money here and there, but somehow somethin' always happened to keep me out of the big winnin's. If I had my rights I ought to be worth plenty. But it's too late now," he sighed. "It's too late for me to start out on the trails again. I ain't young enough now."

The boys were sorry for the old man, but after a while he was quiet and soon his heavy breathing indicated that he had fallen asleep.

"I hope Aunt Gertrude and mother aren't worrying too much," said Frank, as he prepared to undertake first watch.

"It can't be helped," said Joe, wrapping his blanket around him. "We'll be able to get back to-morrow."

"We might take the old man with us," Chet suggested sleepily. "He is pretty well bruised and battered, and he won't be able to live here until the cabin is fixed up again."

"That's a good idea." Frank put another stick of wood in the stove. "You have next watch, Chet. May as well get all the sleep you can."

In a few minutes there was scarcely a sound

in the cottage save the crackling of the fire.
The timbers of the building creaked and
groaned as the night wind hurled itself against
the fragile shelter. Snow slashed against the
roof. Frank Hardy shivered. He was glad
they had obtained even this refuge from the
blizzard

Jadbury Wilson

CHAPTER IV

A TALE OF THE WEST

NEXT morning the storm still raged, and although its fury had somewhat abated the snow was still falling so heavily and the wind was still blowing with such intensity that the boys decided to wait in the shelter of the wrecked cabin in the hope that the blizzard would die down. They were comfortable enough where they were and, after they had eaten breakfast, they even began to enjoy their predicament as an adventure which their school chums would envy.

"The worst of it is," commented Chet, "that to-day is Sunday and we're not getting out of one day of school. Unless," he added, hopefully, "the storm keeps up for another couple of days."

"I don't think it'll be that bad," Frank laughed.

Jadbury Wilson was feeling somewhat more cheerful, although it developed that his bruises and injuries sustained when his house was

blown off the cliff were more serious than had
been at first apparent. No bones were broken,
but he was black and blue in many spots and
unable to rise from his cot without pain.
However, he was philosophic enough to regard
the mishap as part of his lot in life and it was
easily seen that the company of the boys
cheered him up immensely.

"I've had so much bad luck already," he
told them, "that it don't seem like much worse
could ever happen to me."

"What kind of bad luck?" asked Joe, scent-
ing a story.

"All kinds of it," the old man replied.
"When I was out in the West in the early days
it looked at one time as if I'd be a regular
millionaire. And then my bad luck set in and
it's follered me ever since."

"Did you find any mines?" asked Frank.

"In Nevada, we did. Me and my two partners—brothers they were, by the name of Coulson—prospected about for nigh on a year without findin' anything. Then, one day, just
when our grub was runnin' low and it looked
as if we'd have to give up, while I was cuttin'
some firewood for the mornin' my axe-handle
broke and the blade of it went flyin' about a
dozen yards away. When I went over to pick
it up I found it had gone smash against a rock
and chipped some of the surface away."

"And you found gold?" asked Joe eagerly.

"That there little accident uncovered a fine vein of gold. So we started to work it and we staked our property and was gettin' along fine when some smooth strangers heard about it and come out to see what we had. Well, with half an eye they could see we'd made a real find. We was so joyful about it that we didn't try to hide it much. And that's where we made our mistake. You can't trust nobody where gold is concerned."

"What happened?"

"Those smooth chaps went back to town and got a slick lawyer to work with them and one night they come out and jumped our claims. Of course we laughed at 'em, for we knew we'd been there first, but we soon found out what we was up against. That lawyer made out that we hadn't registered our claims right, and he dragged out the case until all our money was gone and we couldn't afford to fight it any longer. And the judge gave a decision against us and we lost our mine."

"Gosh, that was crooked!" remarked Jerry audibly.

"Of course it was crooked! But what could we do? We had to pack up and get out. That there mine was later worth millions, although the joke was on the crooks after all, for their lawyer horned in on the property and worked it so that he got most of it in the long run."

"What did you and the Coulsons do then?"

"We was pretty well discouraged. We just hung around town for a while, but later on we packed up and got clean out of Nevada. We didn't want to be near anythin' that'd remind us of how near we'd been to bein' rich. So we went to Montana."

"Prospecting?"

"Prospectin'. And there we went through all the disappointments of huntin' for gold all over again. We managed to get a fellow to grubstake us and we went out into the mountains and spent almost a whole autumn searchin' high and low for some good ground, but nary a trace of gold did we find. But just as we was about to give up again, Bill Coulson struck it and we figgered that *this* time we would be able to hold on to it. We had a good block of claims and off one of them I got a nugget that prospectors told me was one of the biggest ever seen in that part of the country."

"Well," continued Wilson, "we took mighty good care that we registered our claims *right* that time, and we stayed there all winter and in the spring got down to business. We mined the place ourselves, the three of us. There was a syndicate made us an offer but it didn't seem high enough. A fellow named

Dawson, who had been prospectin' with us for a while in Nevada, showed up at the camp one day, down and out. He had been havin' hard luck too and he was broke, so we took him in with us, for he was a good fellow and he had stood by us when things wasn't goin' well in Nevada."

"Our little mine was all right for a while, but after a time it began to peter out. We had four bags of gold by that time, some of it in big nuggets, but we didn't know whether to cash in and use the money to buy new machinery and sink a deep shaft or not. We were in our camp one night talkin' things over and wonderin' just what to do about it when we heard some one prowlin' around among the rocks.

"I went to the door and opened it, and just then I saw a flash in the dark and then I heard a gun go off. I jumped back into the cabin quick and I could hear the bullet go plunk into the wood at the side of the door. Next minute there was a regular gunfight under way. A gang of toughs from town had heard about our gold and had come up to rob us.

"Well, sir, they surrounded our camp half the night and it looked as if we was out of luck. There was the four bags of gold, everythin' we had in the world, and there was them bandits outside, ready to shoot us if we showed our noses out the door. And our ammunition was givin' out too. We knew we didn't have much chance.

"Finally, Dawson said the only thing to do was for one of us to try and get outside and hide the gold. There was no use hidin' it in the cabin, for they'd be sure to find it. He volunteered to try and reach the mine and hide it underground somewhere. So we figgered it out and decided that was our only chance. Mebbe the bandits might catch him and get the gold, but if we kept it in the cabin they'd be sure to get it anyway, so we figgered we'd better risk it.

"Dawson had lots of nerve. That's one thing I'll say for him although I'll never forgive him for what he done afterward. He had nerve, and somehow I could never believe he really meant to double-cross us at the time. We waited until the shootin' had died down, and along about three o'clock in the mornin', when everythin' was mighty dark, Dawson let himself out the back window. He got out all right, and nobody saw him, and how he ever got through the ring of bandits around the place I never could tell. He had the four bags of gold with him, and mighty heavy they were too. The last we knew, he was creepin' across the rocks toward the shaft. And that was the last we ever saw or heard of him.''

"He ran away?" exclaimed the boys.

"He just cleared out. And he was a fellow any of us would have trusted right to the last. But it only goes to show you can't trust nobody when there's forty or fifty thousand dollars' worth of gold in his hands. We never heard of him again."

"But what about the bandits?"

"After we thought Dawson must have hidden the gold all right, we waited till mornin' and then hung a white handkerchief out the window and gave ourselves up. The bandits came swarmin' in—there was about ten of 'em. One of them was only a young chap, "Black Pepper" they called him, for his real name was Pepperill. He was only a young chap, but a tougher and more cold-blooded fellow I never hope to meet. When they searched the cabin and found that Dawson was gone and the gold with him they was as mad as a nest of hornets. They raved and turned the whole cabin upside down huntin' for that gold, but it didn't do them no good. The gold was gone. So finally they went away, and we set out to hunt for Dawson. But he was gone.

"He wasn't in the mine, although we found footprints down on one of the levels that looked like his, but we couldn't find him anywhere. And there was no gold. Well, even then we couldn't imagine he'd cleared out on us and we

waited around there for nearly a week tryin'
to find him and hopin' he'd show up sometime.
But he never showed up. He had just cleared
out."

"That was a dirty trick!" exclaimed Joe indignantly.

"We didn't mind losin' the gold so much.
It was thinkin' we'd trusted him so much. He
was the last man on earth I'd have thought
would do a thing like that. Bill and Jack Coulson, my pardners, they just *wouldn't* believe it
of him. But after a while we knew we'd never
see him, and although we tried to trace him it
was no use. We heard from a prospector a few
weeks later that he'd seen Dawson in a minin'
camp up North, but that was the last we ever
heard of him. He'd gone up and called him by
name, but Dawson just looked at him kind o'
funny and said he must be mistaken and that
his name wasn't Dawson at all. So I guess
that sort of proved he was crooked."

"And the mine?" asked Frank.

"It wasn't no good after that. We worked
it a few months longer, but it had petered out
and the syndicate wouldn't take a chance on
it and we didn't have any money to work it any
more. So we abandoned it and went away. We
had to split up partnership. I prospected
around Montana five or six years more but
didn't make any more lucky strikes.

"The last I heard of Jack Coulson he was supposed to be dead, and as for Bill he sort of gave up prospectin' and left the mining camps for good. I've never seen either of them since. I went up on a couple of gold rushes in other parts, but I was always too late. I guess it was just my bad luck. I've never had any good luck since. So finally I come East and I've been livin' up here for the last few months, just makin' a living' as best I could. And now look—'' he gestured to the interior of the wrecked cabin. "Bad luck's still follerin' me.''

The boys gazed at the old man in silence. His story of misfortune had made a profound impression upon them. Ill-luck had certainly pursued him relentlessly.

"The storm's dyin' down,'' said Jadbury Wilson at last. "You'll be goin' back to the city, I guess.''

"But how about you?'' asked Frank.

"I'll just have to stay here and make the best of it. I can build a new cabin, but I'm not goin' to build it on top of the cliff this time. I'll build it back in the wood where the worst that can happen is havin' a tree fall on it.''

"But you won't be able to work for a few days yet,'' Joe pointed out.

"That's true,'' admitted the old man. "I can't even get up off this cot right now.''

"You'll have to come to town with us. Have you got a sled here that we could draw you in on?"

"I got a sled all right. But what's the use? There's no place for me to go when I do get into town. I ain't got no money."

"You can stay at our place," declared Frank. "I know mother won't mind. You can stay there until you get on your feet again."

"I'm sure it's mighty good of you," said Wilson gratefully. "But I don't like to be intrudin' on people."

The old man's simple independence won the boys' admiration. But Frank and Joe knew it would be impossible to leave him alone in the wrecked cabin in his present condition. It was unthinkable.

"You'll come with us," Frank said, with determination. "Let's get the sled ready fellows."

CHAPTER V

Con Riley Under Fire

THE blizzard died down as suddenly as it began, and when the Hardy boys and their chums
left the cabin they found that the snow had
ceased falling and that the sun was shining
brightly.

They found Jadbury Wilson's long sled tied
to the outside of one of the cabin walls. It had
been unharmed, and it did not take the boys
long to place blankets upon it and make the old
man comfortable. They had to assist him out
of the cabin, so greatly did his injuries pain
him. He had two pair of snowshoes, and Chet
Morton and Jerry Gilroy donned them, the
Hardy boys being content to trudge along in
the deep snow of the lake.

In a short time they had left the cabin and
were making their way toward Willow River,
pausing frequently to rest because the deep
snow soon wearied them. However, when they
reached the river they found that they made
better progress because the stream was pro-

tected by high wooded banks and the snow had
not drifted as deeply as on the lake. But it
was mid-afternoon before they reached the
road leading into Bayport.

From there on their progress was easy, and,
dragging the sled with Jadbury Wilson
wrapped in his blankets, they at length reached
the Hardy home on High Street. Here they
were all welcomed by Mrs. Hardy and Aunt
Gertrude, who had been frantic with anxiety
concerning the boys' whereabouts.

"We were going to send out a searching
party for you!" exclaimed Mrs. Hardy, as she
kissed her sons and sent Chet and Jerry in to
telephone to their parents the news of their
arrival.

"I knew they'd get lost. I told them so!"
declared Aunt Gertrude vigorously. But if she
had a scolding in store for them she soon forgot it in her immediate concern over Jadbury
Wilson, whom Chet and Jerry brought into the
house.

When the Hardy boys explained the situation and told of their adventures and the
reason for their delay, Mrs. Hardy was insistent that Jadbury Wilson should make his
home with them until he could be on his feet
again.

"You'll certainly have to stay with us!" she
said. "There's plenty of room."

"I'm sure I'm most thankful to you, ma'am," said the old prospector humbly.

As for Aunt Gertrude, she was already scurrying about the kitchen making hot ginger for the new guest and when it was ready she stood over Jadbury Wilson until he had drunk the last drop.

Then the boys put him to bed, and as the old man relaxed into the warm blankets he sighed and remarked that it was the first time in five years that he had experienced the comforts of a soft mattress.

Jerry and Chet hastened home, wondering a little what would be said to them. But their people were so relieved at seeing them again that they forbore to lecture the lads, and, all in all, they came through the ordeal better than they had expected.

"Back to school to-morrow!" grumbled Joe, at supper that night.

"Oh, didn't I tell you?" said Mrs. Hardy.

"Tell us what?"

"There won't be any school to-morrow."

"What?" shouted the boys incredulously.

"You should say, 'I beg your pardon?'" corrected Aunt Gertrude acidly.

Mrs. Hardy smiled.

"I thought you'd be surprised," she said. "And I suppose you'll be almost heartbroken. No, there's to be no school to-morrow. Last night's blizzard was one of the worst in the history of Bayport. The wind was so strong that it wrecked the high school roof.''

Joe gave a whoop of delight and danced around his chair.

"There's nothing to cheer about that I can see," sniffed Aunt Gertrude. "They say the property damage was very bad and it will take about two weeks before the roof is fixed.''

The news proved too much for the Hardy boys. Like most youths of their age, the unexpected prospect of a winter holiday filled them with delight. Mrs. Hardy smiled at them indulgently, for she had not forgotten her own schooldays.

Aunt Gertrude began laying down the law to the effect that the boys must pursue their studies at home quite as ardently as though the school had been undamaged, and on the following day she actually did insist that they do two hours' studying before they got out in the morning.

When the boys finally made their escape and raced to the nearest hillside with their bobsleds they found most of the students of the Bayport high school already there. Tony Prito, Phil Cohen, Biff Hooper, Chet Morton and Jerry Gilroy were on hand, as well as many of the girls.

Callie Shaw, of whom Frank Hardy was an

ardent admirer, and Iola Morton, sister of
Chet and the only girl who had ever won an
approving glance from Joe Hardy, were hilari-
ously bobsledding and looking unusually pretty
in gaily colored sweaters and woollen toques,
their eyes sparkling and their cheeks flushed
with the cold.

For half an hour or more the sliding continued, the boys having the time of their lives,
and then Nemesis appeared on the scene in the
person of Officer Con Riley.

Now, as old readers know, Riley was the
sworn enemy of the youth of Bayport. A stolid,
thick-set individual with more dignity and self-
importance than brains, he took the responsi-
bilities of his position on the Bayport police
force very seriously. He had the view, too
common to the type of elderly people who have
forgotten that they once were young, that all
enjoyment is sinful and that all young people
are continually up to mischief.

So, when Con Riley saw the merry party on
the hillside he recollected an ancient and obso-
lete city ordinance forbidding bobsledding else-
where than in the parks. This ordinance had
originally been passed to prevent youngsters
sliding down hills adjacent to the trolley tracks
and thereby endangering their lives. The fact
that there were no trolley tracks near this particular hill mattered nothing to Officer Riley.

Majestically he stood at the bottom of the hill and held up his hand. Sled after sled pulled to a stop and Officer Riley, the personification of the majesty of the law, ordered the fun to cease.

There was nothing to be done. Officer Riley had the authority, and he knew it.

"Well," said Chet Morton grimly, "we'll just have to have our fun some other way. Let's have a snowball fight."

Officer Riley looked dubious and produced a little notebook which he perused earnestly. He knew Chet Morton and his mischievous proclivities of old. But although he looked through the rules and regulations hopefully he could find nothing to prohibit snowballing. However, he withdrew to the street and paced slowly up and down in the faint hope that perhaps a stray snowball might break a near-by window, in which case he would have a delicious opportunity to interfere once more with the sport.

Chet gathered his cohorts and talked earnestly for a few minutes. Then, with many giggles, his followers set to work building two snow forts directly opposite one another. The forts were merely rude snow embankments, just sufficient to provide protection for the opposing sides. Then the young people began rolling snowballs.

So far, so good. Officer Riley was unable to

detect anything wrong in this. Still, the fight had not started. There was still the hope of a shattered window pane.

Majestically, he paced to and fro, keeping a wary eye on the snow forts and the gaily clad figures behind the banks. Then, to his surprise, he saw Chet Morton walking slowly toward him.

Officer Riley eyed Chet suspiciously. The fact did not escape him that Chet had one hand behind his back.

"Aha!" he muttered. "A snowball."

He was right.

Hardly had the suspicion crossed his mind than it became a frigid reality.

Chet seemed to aim at one of the forts. But his foot appeared to slip and the snowball smacked Con Riley's helmet with deadly accuracy, knocking it off into the snow.

Riley emitted a roar of rage and astonishment. Snow was trickling down his neck. He stooped merely long enough to pick up his helmet and thrust it back on his head, where it rested at a ridiculous and rather precarious angle.

Then he gave chase to the rash youth who had thus tempted his wrath.

Chet went ploughing through the snow, directly in between the forts. Con Riley plunged recklessly in pursuit. Even yet he did not suspect the trick, did not suspect that Chet was merely luring him on to destruction.

Not until a second snowball whizzed past his head, not until a third smacked wetly against his ear, did he realize that he had plunged neatly into a trap.

He floundered about in snow up to his knees, and from either side came a volley of snowballs. They squashed against his helmet, knocking it off again, they thumped against his uniform on every side. No matter which way he turned, flying snowballs met him. And the boys took good care to keep their faces out of sight.

"Stop it!" he roared.

But the merciless bombardment continued.

He made a frantic rush toward one of the forts, but the snow was too deep to permit of rapid progress and the air seemed full of white missiles. One snowball caught him in the eye and stopped his rush momentarily. He wavered. More snowballs caught him in the rear. He turned around and a concerted bombardment opened up from each fort. Officer Riley decided that discretion was the better part of valor and he ignominiously retreated.

As for Chet Morton, he was safely ensconced behind a particularly heavy snowbank, laughing until the tears came to his eyes. When next he peeped out he saw that Officer Riley, having retrieved his precious helmet, was making great speed back toward the comparative safety of the sidewalk. With the greatest dignity that he could command under the circumstances, he brushed the snow off his uniform. Then, sadly, he resumed his beat, and headed toward the downtown part of Bayport, where citizens were more law-abiding and where snowballs were unknown.

The Hardy boys and their chums saw their enemy disappear around the block, and then Chet rose to the top of the ramparts and gave a cheer of victory.

" 'We have met the enemy and they are ours!' " he quoted.

A snowball from the opposite fort struck him on the ear and he sat down abruptly.

Then the fight began in earnest. It was not until Chet had personally led his warriors out of their fortress and across the no man's land between to win a glorious victory over the other army and had personally washed the face of the marksman who had ruined his triumphant cheers that peace was restored. Then, the forts having been demolished, the bobsleds were pressed into service again, and the hill rang with shouts and laughter until nightfall. For Officer Con Riley made it his business to attend to duties downtown for the rest of the day.

CHAPTER VI

A Message from Montana

WHEN the Hardy boys returned home that night after their afternoon's fun and sat down to an ample hot dinner of steak and onions, with mashed potatoes, thick gravy "and all the trimmings," as Jadbury Wilson expressed it, they found that the old miner had won a firm place in the household. He was able to be up and around again, although he hobbled painfully about, but his tales of the early days in the mining country of the West had won the interest of the women.

Mrs. Hardy was particularly interested when he talked of Montana, because of the fact that her husband was in that particular state at the time.

As for Aunt Gertrude, she was in a constant condition of solicitous excitement seeing that the old man was comfortable. And comfortable he was. It was a treat to see him relax in an easy chair after dinner, puffing contentedly at the pipe that he never allowed out of his sight.

In the evening Frank and Joe besought him to tell again the story of how he had been so basely cheated of his fortune in the West, and the women listened entranced to the strange tale.

"Do you mean to tell me that that wicked man actually ran away with all the gold you had worked for so hard?" exclaimed Aunt Gertrude indignantly.

"Looks that way, ma'am!"

"The scoundrel! I just wish I had him here for a minute. I'd tell him a few things!"

"I'd tell him a few things myself," said Wilson mildly. "Still, it was a great many years ago and there's no use thinkin' about it now. The gold's gone and I'm an old man."

"It's a shame!" said Mrs. Hardy.

"I guess I couldn't have been much use as a prospector, or I'd have been able to hold on to what I got," observed Wilson. "I've come to the conclusion that a man gets pretty much what he deserves in this world. If he ain't smart enough to hold on to what he's got, he deserves to lose it."

"Didn't you make anything out of your mining days at all?" put in Frank.

"Oh—a few dollars here and a few dollars there. Enough to keep me in grub and with a place to sleep. Once in a while I'd make some extra money, but it never lasted long somehow.

I got a claim out in Montana yet, so far as that goes.''

"Is it worth anything?"

Jadbury Wilson shrugged and stroked his beard.

"Maybe worth much—maybe worth nothing," he said.

"Can't you find out?"

"I haven't got enough money to work the property. It's the only claim I've been able to pay my dues on, all these years. But I kept payin' 'em, sort of hoping somethin' would turn up some day. I've always thought it *should* be a good claim. It's in a good location. But I've never had enough money ahead to do any more work on it."

"Can't you get any one to finance you?" asked Joe.

"Not me," sighed the old man. "All through Montana I got the reputation of bein' too unlucky. They're afraid to take a chance on me any more. They say, 'Why, that's Jad Wilson's claim. Even if it is good, he's always been so all-fired unlucky that we'll be bound to lose our money!' So they pass it up."

"Never mind. Perhaps you'll come into your own some day," said Mrs. Hardy comfortingly.

"It'll have to come mighty soon, then," replied the old man, with a wry smile. "I've waited so long now that it seems I'll be dead and gone before my luck starts to turn."

However, under the influence of the warm fire and the cheerful company his natural optimism manifested itself and he was soon entertaining his new-found friends with stories both humorous and tragic of his adventures in the early days of the rough-and-ready mining camps of the West.

"I'd love to go out there!" said Joe wistfully.

"It ain't all beer and skittles," said Jadbury Wilson. "There's quite a bit of adventure, but there's a lot of rough livin' and mighty skimpy eatin' at times. I've often seen the day when all my flour and beans would be gone and the grocer wouldn't trust me for another nickel's worth. And, of course, the West has changed a lot nowadays. It's got mighty civilized, they tell me."

"Our father is out in Montana now," Frank remarked.

"You don't say! And whereabouts in Montana is he?"

"He's at a mining camp. It's a queer-sounding place called Lucky Bottom."

Jad Wilson's eyes widened.

"Lucky Bottom!" he exclaimed. "Can you beat that?"

"Why?"

"Lucky Bottom is right near the place where Bart Dawson run away with all our gold."

"Isn't that a strange coincidence!" ejaculated Mrs. Hardy.

"It shore is," agreed Jad Wilson. "Mighty strange. To think that he should be in the very place where we lost our fortune. It's a small world, ain't it?"

"What kind of place is Lucky Bottom?" asked Frank.

"It ain't very big. In the old days it was a real rough-and-ready minin' camp, with dance-halls and saloons. Then, as the mines got worked out and the miners went on up into the copper fields, the town sort of dwindled away. It's a sort of ghost camp nowadays, I guess. Nobody there but a couple of store-keepers and a few miners who keep pluggin' away still hopin' to find some gold that somebody else has missed."

Jadbury Wilson rubbed his eyes and smothered a yawn.

"You'll have to pardon me, ma'am," he said to Mrs. Hardy, "but I've always been used to goin' to bed at dark and it ain't often I sit up so late jawin'. If you don't mind, I think I'll turn in."

"'Early to bed and early to rise—,'" quoted Aunt Gertrude, with approval.

"'Makes a man healthy and wealthy and

wise,' " finished Jadbury Wilson, with a wry smile. "Well, I been gettin' up early and goin' to bed early all my life and it's never made me wealthy and I'm mighty sure I ain't very wise. About all it's done is to make me healthy. You couldn't kill me if you belted me over the head with a church."

He bade them good-night and went upstairs to bed. Aunt Gertrude remarked that the Hardy boys would be well-advised to follow the old man's example in the matter of early retirement, but they sat up for almost an hour before the fire, talking over some of the yarns the old miner had recounted.

"He sure had some great experiences," said Frank, before they went to sleep that night.

"You bet he did. I wish we could get out there for a while."

"It probably wouldn't be the same now. He said the country has got pretty tame."

"It can't be so tame when they have to call dad out there in their gold-stealing cases. There must be some excitement left."

"Oh, well, there's not much chance of us getting out that far to find out. Go to sleep."

But in the morning a surprise awaited them. When they came down to breakfast they found Mrs. Hardy already at the table, perusing a yellow sheet of paper.

"Telegram?" said Frank.

Mrs. Hardy nodded.

"It's from your father."

"Is he coming back?"

"Not yet. As a matter of fact, he wants you boys to go out to him at once."

Frank and Joe looked at one another incredulously. The news seemed too good to be true. Mrs. Hardy handed over the telegram.

It read:

"Please let Frank and Joe come to me at once. Will send special word and instructions to Majestic Hotel, Chicago.

"Fenton Hardy."

"What on earth can this call mean?" exclaimed Frank, in complete amazement.

"I can't understand it at all," admitted their mother. She was frankly worried.

"I don't care whether I understand it or not," said Joe. "It means he wants us to go out West, and that's enough for me. When can we start?"

"The telegram says 'at once,' " Mrs. Hardy remarked. "It seems very strange. And so sudden, too. I wonder what on earth he can want you for?"

"Perhaps he needs our help on that case he's working on," Frank suggested.

Aunt Gertrude, who had hitherto taken no part in the discussion, sniffed audibly.

The Hardy boys were so excited that they could hardly eat their breakfast. All through the meal they jubilantly discussed details of the proposed trip and when Mrs. Hardy, although admittedly worried at the prospect of letting them go so far by themselves, agreed that they might go immediately, as the telegram suggested, they flung themselves into a feverish orgy of packing.

Jadbury Wilson was highly interested and gave them a number of excellent suggestions as to what they should take with them on the trip.

"Lots of good, heavy underclothes and plenty of woolen socks," he said. "You'll find it plenty colder out there than it is here."

The boys got their reservations on a train that would leave for Chicago late that afternoon. Their packing occupied more time than they had expected because they did not want to be burdened by too much luggage and had a difficult time eliminating the nonessentials At last, however, they were ready. Aunt Gertrude, who had kept up a running fire of instructions and admonitions concerning their conduct on the journey, and who freely predicted disaster in the shape of train wrecks and robbers, gave them her final instructions. Mrs. Hardy, who merely kissed them good-bye and told them to write to her as soon as they

reached Chicago, called a taxi to take them to
the station, and Jadbury Wilson, warning them
to be on the lookout for "them city slickers in
Chicago" and advising them not to talk to
strangers, told them not to worry inasmuch as
he would look after their mother and Aunt
Gertrude.

The taxi arrived. The luggage was tossed in.
The boys scrambled into the back seat. Aunt
Gertrude shrieked "Good-bye" a dozen times
and sobbed audibly. Their mother waved a
handkerchief. Jadbury Wilson brandished his
cane. Then, with a roar, the taxi sped down
the street and headed toward the station. Already the boys could hear the long-drawn
whistle of the train.

"Off for Montana!" exclaimed Frank.

"I'm afraid of only one thing," remarked
his brother.

"What's that?"

"I'm afraid I'll wake up and find I've been
dreaming."

CHAPTER VII

In the Windy City

THE Hardy boys had never been on a long train journey before, and the trip, consequently, was replete with interest for them. As the train left Bayport behind and began speeding through the open country with its snow-covered fields, they felt a sense of elation and freedom.

"This is certainly better than school!" declared Joe, settling back in his seat with a sigh of contentment.

"Sure is. Chet Morton and the rest of the gang will be just about sick with envy when they hear where we've gone."

"I wish we could have them with us. When do we reach Chicago?"

"Some time to-morrow. Won't it be dandy to stay on the train all night!"

They watched the scenery that seemed to dash past as though on a moving scroll until gradually twilight fell and the lights in the Pullman were turned on. They went into the dining car, where they were served a massive dinner with an air of elaborate courtesy. The novelty of eating an excellent and perfectly served dinner while speeding swiftly across country appealed to them, and when they had finally risen to their feet and left a tip for the waiter, Joe was of the opinion that he could imagine nothing better than living this way all the time.

"When I grow up, if I have money enough, I'll just live on the trains," he said solemnly.

"You'd soon get tired of it."

"Not me!" And not until the novelty of the long journey began to wear off did Joe admit to himself that possibly such an existence might be wearisome in the long run.

They slept the sound slumber of healthy youth and were up early next morning for the first breakfast call. There, at their table with its immaculate linen and gleaming silverware, they did justice to crisp bacon and golden eggs, the meanwhile looking out the wide windows at the murky chimneys and dark masses of factory buildings as the train entered the outskirts of a large city. The train roared across viaducts and they could see trolleys and automobiles speeding to and fro in the city streets in bewildering confusion. For the first time they began to have some appreciation of the real extent of their country.

"I guess Bayport isn't the only city in the States," said Frank, with a smile.

"It looks pretty small compared to some of these that we've gone through."

But as the morning passed they wearied at last of looking at the scenery, varied as it was, and toward mid-afternoon they began to be impatient for a sight of Chicago. When, at last, the train began to roar through the suburbs of the Windy City, as a friendly porter called it when they had failed to understand his reference to it as "Chi," they felt a mounting excitement. But the train rushed in past seemingly endless rows of houses, then past miles of industrial buildings overhung with a cloud of murky smoke, until they thought the center of the city would never be reached.

The journey came finally to an end. Their porter was on the platform with their grips, they tipped him for his services during the trip and made their way down the crowded pavement, through the gates into the concourse of the enormous station. Here they gazed about in frank wonderment at the bustling hordes of people, all intent on their own affairs, moving to and from the trains. The constant sound of shuffling feet, buzzing voices, clanging bells, all the varied noises of a great railway station. sounded like the roar of the ocean in their ears.

They made their way outside and clambered into a waiting taxi, directing the driver to take them to the hotel their father had mentioned in his telegram. In a short time the car drew up at the entrance, after a brief ride through crowded, noisy streets that made the main street of Bayport seem like a country lane on Sunday afternoon by comparison. A bellboy seized their grips and the boys presented themselves at the desk.

The clerk glanced at their names after they had signed.

"Ah, yes!" he said. "Frank and Joe Hardy. Your room has been reserved for you. And there is also a letter, I believe." He reached into a pigeon-hole in a compartment near by and produced a letter which he tossed over to them. He struck a bell smartly. "Front! Show these gentlemen to 845."

Feeling highly important at being referred to as "gentlemen" and at having a bedroom actually reserved for them in a hotel of such grandeur, the Hardy boys followed a military looking bellboy to the elevators, whence followed a swift ascent to the eighth floor. Then down wide, silent corridors to their room, a substantial, bright and airy room with bath It was all a revelation to the lads, who had never been in a big hotel before, and when they looked out the big windows down on the thronging life of the city streets below they were excited beyond measure.

"First of all, we'll read dad's letter," said Frank. "These are the instructions he promised, I suppose."

He opened the envelope and read:

"My Dear Boys:

"I could have given you all the instructions that were necessary in the telegram I sent to your mother, but I thought it best that you come to Chicago first and have a little rest before resuming your journey. This would also give me a chance to tell you more about the mission I have decided to send you on. The truth of the matter is, I have been hurt, and am now laid up in a miner's cabin and have been unable to continue my investigations in the case I have in hand. For this reason I am calling on you to help me, for I think I can trust to your abilities by now by reason of the assistance you have given me in other cases. I did not want to worry your mother needlessly, which is the reason I did not mention my injury. It is not serious but it will be some time before I am able to be on my feet again, and, in the meanwhile, time is precious.

"In my investigations here I have discovered a secret concerning some stolen gold. It is this matter that I wish you to investigate for me. To do so it will be necessary for you to come to Lucky Bottom, Montana, at once. Have a good night's rest at the hotel and then come on here. I am under the care of a miner by the name of Hank Shale, and when you reach Lucky Bottom any one will be able to tell you where to find his place. I shall be expecting you, so do not fail me. I hope you have a pleasant trip. Do not worry about me, as I am in good hands and progressing favorably.

"Your dad,

"Fenton Hardy."

Frank put down the letter, with a low whistle. "So that's the reason he called for us!" he said. "Dad's been hurt."

"He says it isn't very serious."

"It's serious enough when it means he's not able to be on his feet. Perhaps we ought to start out to him right away."

"Not much use of that," objected Joe. "We wouldn't gain much time and we'd be so tired when we got there that we wouldn't be of much use to him for a day or so. I think we'd better rest here to-night, as he suggests, and go on to-morrow."

Frank considered his brother's advice sound, and, after enjoying a good dinner, the boys went out and wandered about the busy streets for almost an hour, enjoying the sights of the Windy City. But it was a cold, bitter evening, and they soon sought the warmth and comfort of their hotel again, going to bed early, because they were tired after their long hours on the train.

They were told by the information clerk that their train would leave at eleven o'clock the following morning. This gave them plenty of time for a good sleep, a bath and a leisurely breakfast. When all their preparations for the continuation of the journey had been made they presented themselves at the desk in the lobby to check out. Frank paid the bill, and the boys were just about to move away from the desk when a neat, elderly man somewhat below medium height, came up to him.

"Are you the Hardy boys?" he asked, glancing quizzically at them.

"Yes."

"I was told to be on the lookout for you," said the elderly man. "My name is Hopkins."

"Who sent you, Mr. Hopkins?" asked Frank politely.

"I am your father's lawyer—that is, in Chicago," said the neat little man. "He sent me a telegram last night asking me to look you up here and do what I could for you. I have arranged for your transportation as far as

Lucky Bottom. That's where you are bound, isn't it?"

"Yes, that's the place."

"Well, then," said Mr. Hopkins, "if you'll come with me I'll see that your accommodations are ready for you. I made the arrangements with the railway this morning."

Reflecting that they were certainly obtaining first-class service on their trip across country, the Hardy boys accompanied Mr. Hopkins across the lobby and out to the street, where a taxi was waiting. The porter put their luggage inside and Mr. Hopkins got in with them, directing the driver to the station.

"Your father is an old friend of mine," said the lawyer, "and I'm only too glad to be of service to his sons. I handle a great deal of his Chicago business for him."

Although the Hardy boys had not been aware that their father had a great deal of Chicago business, they were properly appreciative of Mr. Hopkins' kindness, and when they finally reached the station and he guided them through the gates to the train they expressed their thanks for what he had done for them.

"It's nothing—nothing," he said brusquely.

"We can hardly look at it that way," replied Frank.

Mr. Hopkins, absorbed in the details for the

boys' comfort, did not answer. Instead he turned and said:

"Porter—how about Compartment B?"

"All ready, sir! All ready!" the porter assured him, leading them to the compartment. "All ready, sir, just as you asked."

"We're traveling in style," murmured Frank, nudging his brother.

CHAPTER VIII

The Second Stranger

Mr. Hopkins bustled about the compartment, making everything comfortable for the Hardy boys and chatting affably.

"You'll be looked after right until you reach Montana," he said. "You won't have to change trains. There'll be no bother."

"We're very grateful to you—" began Frank.

The little lawyer dismissed their thanks with a gesture.

"It's no trouble at all," he said. "No trouble at all. Your father would do as much for me any day."

From out on the platform they heard the stentorian cry, "All Aboard!" Mr. Hopkins glanced at his watch.

"I'll have to go," he said quickly. Then, without waiting to say good-bye, he dashed out of the compartment, slamming the door behind him in his haste.

The Hardy boys settled back in the comfort

able seats as the train began to move. They looked out the window as they emerged from the great train-shed and then they were occupied gazing at the city streets as the locomotive picked up speed and roared on its way.

In due time the train passed through the outskirts of Chicago, then it rushed on through open stretches of country, past little towns and villages. It was an express that evidently stopped only at the larger cities.

"At this rate it won't take us long to reach Montana," Frank remarked.

"We're sure making good time."

"What do you say to going out and sitting in the observation car for a while?" Frank suggested. "It's roomier than this compartment."

"Suits me."

Frank went to the door. To his surprise he found that it would not open. He tried again, but the door refused to budge.

"That's funny," he remarked. "We're locked in."

Both the boys tried the door, but it was of no avail.

"The catch must have been on when Mr. Hopkins went out," Frank said. Even yet the real truth of the situation had not dawned on them.

They hammered on the door for a while, but

no one heard them. At last Frank caught sight
of the bell button.

"That's stupid of me," he said, with a smile.
"I should have known there'd be a bell to call
the porter."

He pressed the button and waited. No one
came. There was no sound but the roar of the
train as it rushed on its way. He pressed the
button again and again.

"That porter must be either dead or asleep,"
he muttered, settling down to a prolonged ring-
ing of the bell.

After what seemed an interminable length
of time they heard a shuffling of feet in the
corridor. The sound of the steps ceased, and
some one rapped at the door.

"Something for you, gentlemen?"

"Yes—let us out of here!"

The porter tried the handle of the door.

"By golly," he observed, "you locked yourselves in."

"We didn't lock ourselves in. Somebody
locked us in. Haven't you got a key?"

"Just a minute."

They heard the porter shuffling away. After
a while he returned with the sleeping car conductor, a key clicked in the lock, and then the
door swung open.

"How on earth did that happen?" asked the
conductor, mystified. He looked at the porter

accusingly. "Did you lock these boys in there?"

"No, sir! No, sir!" protested the porter. "I didn't have anything to do with it, sir! They came on at Chicago with an older man and I showed them to their compartment and that's all I know about it."

"I don't think the porter had anything to do with our being locked in," explained Frank. "It was an accident. Our friend Mr. Hopkins slammed the door on his way out and the catch must have been on without our knowing it. It's perfectly all right."

"I got their tickets all right," said the conductor.

"Yes, sir. I collected their tickets myself. The old man with these boys gave them to me. Two tickets to Indianapolis."

"To where?" asked Frank, in amazement.

"Indianapolis."

"But we're not going to Indianapolis."

"That's what your tickets say."

The Hardy Boys looked at one another in consternation.

"But we're going to Montana. Didn't Mr. Hopkins give you tickets to Lucky Bottom, Montana?"

The conductor produced some tickets from his pocket and glanced through them. "Even if he did," he remarked, "they wouldn't be any use on this train. We're bound south, not west. No," he concluded, "your tickets are here, Compartment B, and they read Indianapolis."

"We've been tricked!" declared Frank hotly. "Mr. Hopkins said he had been sent to look after us and that this train would take us right through to Montana."

"And then he locked the door on you so you wouldn't go around making inquiries until it was too late," added the conductor. "Your friend certainly put one over on you. But I'm afraid we can't do much for you now. We're quite a distance out of Chicago, and this train doesn't stop for another hour yet."

"Another hour!"

"That's the best we can do."

"Well," said Frank, disgusted, "I guess we'll just have to wait and get off at the first stop, and then take the next train back to Chicago. This will hold us up another day on our trip."

"Sorry," said the conductor sympathetically. "Of course it isn't our fault. We couldn't know you were supposed to be going West."

"No, of course not. It was Hopkins. He planned the whole thing from the start. Oh, well!" Frank shrugged. "We might as well wait."

He and Joe went back into the compartment and sat down again. This unexpected development left them silent and discouraged. Too late now, they saw that the astute Hopkins had deliberately sought to prevent them from joining their father in Montana. He had worked the trick very neatly, and it might easily have happened that the boys would not have discovered the deception until they reached Indianapolis had it not been for the chance remark of the porter. For that, at least, they were thankful.

"Dad's enemies mustn't be very anxious to have us reach Montana, if they'll go to these lengths to sidetrack us," said Joe, at last.

"We'll get there if we have to walk," Frank replied grimly.

They had no further enjoyment of the scenery. Each flitting telegraph pole meant that they were drawing farther away from Chicago and losing so much more time in resuming their journey to the West. At length the train began to slow down and, looking out, they saw that they were approaching a small railway town with an immense water tank.

The porter came to the door of the compartment.

"Here's the first stop," he told them. "You can get a train back to Chicago from here!"

He took their luggage and, when the train

came to a stop, the boys got out onto the platform.

"Now I wonder how long we'll have to wait before we get a train back," remarked Frank.

His eye caught a bulletin board in front of the little station and he went over to it. At length he found what he sought, a late train bound for Chicago, and he almost groaned as he noted the time.

"There won't be a train along for five hours," he reported to Joe.

"Good-night!"

"That means we've got to cool our heels around here until dark. Five solid hours."

Dolefully, they confronted the bulletin board. A young man in a heavy ulster and tweed cap was also studying it. He glanced toward them.

"What's the trouble?" he asked.

"Isn't there any earlier train to Chicago than that?"

The young man shook his head.

"I'm afraid not," he said. "I guess you're out of luck. In a hurry to get there?"

Frank nodded.

"That's too bad. But say—," the young man reflected a moment. "If you motored over to Greendale you'd be able to catch an earlier train. There's another railroad passes through there."

"If we can catch an earlier train, that's the

train we want," said Frank decidedly. "How far away is Greendale and how do we get there?"

"It's about twenty miles across country. I'm motoring over there myself right now. You're welcome to come along with me if you wish. I'm just waiting until the line is clear so I can put through a telephone call."

"Do you think we can make the train at Greendale all right?"

"Oh, yes. I'm sure of it. There's a train leaves for Chicago in about an hour and we'll be there in plenty of time. There's my car beside the platform. Put your grips in it and I'll be along in a few minutes."

The young man went into the waiting room and the Hardy boys saw him go into a telephone booth to put through his call. Frank and Joe, congratulating themselves on this lucky turn of events that had saved them from a dreary five-hour wait, went over to the touring car the young man had indicated and put their grips in the back seat. In about five minutes their new-found friend emerged from the waiting room.

"All set?" he asked. "I made inquiries about your train and you'll be able to make it all right. Hop in."

He insisted that they sit in the front seat with him as there was plenty of room. "I

like company when I'm driving," he said cheerfully, and this removed the last vestige of re-
luctance in the Hardy boys' minds, as they had
been slightly afraid that they might be proving
themselves bothersome to the stranger.

He was a skilful driver and the roads were
good. The big touring car sped along the highway and they left the village behind, racing
out into the open country. The young man at
the wheel said little, beyond an occasional remark about the weather or the condition of the
roads.

Not until they were at least ten miles from
the town did the boys have a suspicion that
anything might be wrong. That was when the
young man turned the car suddenly off the
main highway down a lonely road. The car
lurched heavily to and fro in the deep ruts.

"I thought you said the other town was on
the main highway," said Frank.

"I know the way," retorted the man at the
wheel gruffly.

Something in his tone made the Hardy boys
suspicious. Frank glanced at his brother and
he could tell by his expression that Joe did not
like the situation either.

Some distance ahead they saw an object
parked directly across the road. It was an
automobile, and it effectually blocked their
passage.

"Somebody wrecked, I guess," said their driver carelessly. He began to slow down. Frank, who was on the outside of the seat, groped under the flap in the door until his fingers encountered a heavy wrench. He was not going to be caught altogether unprepared.

The car came to a stop. From around the front of the other automobile came three unsavory individuals, unshaven, with peaked caps pulled low over their foreheads.

"Now," said the young man beside them, suddenly whipping out a pistol, "you'll just come along with us."

He leveled the weapon directly at the Hardy boys.

CHAPTER IX

THE ESCAPE

FRANK HARDY wasted not a second.

Before the man with the automatic pistol could realize what he was doing, he had flung up his hands sharply, at the same time releasing his grip on the wrench. It spun straight and true, knocking the automatic out of the fellow's grasp and it clattered to the floor of the car.

When Joe saw that their antagonist was unarmed he rose halfway up in the seat and launched himself upon the driver. Frank, in the meantime, reached for the pistol. He was unable to find it, but his fingers closed over the wrench again.

There was a yell of surprise and rage from the three men in the road and they rushed toward the car. One of them came plunging along the side and attempted to grapple with Frank, but a sideways swing of the wrench caught him on the right of the head and he staggered back with a yelp of pain.

75

Joe was still struggling with the driver of the car. The latter was at a disadvantage in that he had been caught unawares. The loss of his automatic had flustered him and Joe's sudden onslaught had taken him completely by surprise. Penned in by the wheel, he was unable to use his superior weight to advantage, and Joe seemed all over him, pounding him unmercifully.

One of the other toughs leaned over the side and seized Joe by the back of the coat. The man who had been hit with the wrench was dancing about in pain and keeping at a respectful distance. The other fellow was attempting to close in on Frank. He sprang forward, just dodged a sweeping blow of the wrench, and then wrestled with the boy.

They swayed to and fro. The tough was of husky build and his gorilla-like arms were possessed of great strength. The door of the car flew open and the pair staggered from the running board into the roadway. They rolled about, fighting and struggling, while the man who had been hit with the wrench took occasion to deliver a vicious kick at Frank. A sudden twist, however, brought the other man into range at the moment and he received the kick that was intended for the boy.

But the Hardys were outnumbered. Joe was quickly overcome and the other pair would soon have beaten Frank into submission but for a surprising interruption.

Down the roadway came a clattering and roaring, and around the other car came plunging an ancient and decrepit Ford with an enormous man at the wheel. Beside him sat another large man, and the pair gazed at the struggle before them, with mouths agape and eyes staring. Then the man driving the car brought it to a stop and clambered down, picking up the car crank as he went.

"You're the speeders that ran over my chickens!" he roared, bearing down on the two toughs who were grappling with Frank. He dealt one of them a hearty rap on the back of the head with the crank, and the fellow bolted forthwith. Reinforcements had arrived, and he judged that the fight would soon be over. He raced for the car parked across the road and scrambled into the front seat.

The two large men rushed into the battle with enthusiasm. The three toughs in the other car had, it appeared, deliberately driven their automobile into a flock of chickens at the side of the road near the chicken farm farther down the road. Revenge, therefore, was sweet.

In a very short time the fight was at an end. The toughs broke and fled, regained their car, and were soon careening down the road. As for the young man who had brought the Hardy boys into this trap, he managed to get his own car started, shook off his attackers, and the automobile plunged forward.

"Let them go," said Frank, picking himself up out of the ditch.

"If they run over any more of my chickens, I'll follow them from here till Doomsday," declared the angry farmer.

"You certainly showed up in the nick of time," said Joe, brushing off his coat. "They had us beaten, two to one."

"They're no good!" declared the other man. "I know 'em. They're nothing but poolroom toughs."

"How come they were waiting for you 'way out here?" asked the driver.

"The man driving the touring car was going to drive us out to a town called Greendale so we could get a train back to Chicago," Frank explained, and told the man where they had got into the automobile. "He turned down this road, and then we met the other three waiting for us. They all jumped us at once."

"No trains pass through Greendale," declared their rescuer. "If you wait there for a train for Chicago, you'll wait years and years, and even then you won't get a train for *anywhere*."

"We'll have to go back to the station then," said Joe.

"That's where we're headed. Get in our car and we'll drive you back."

Glad to have gotten out of the scrape this easily, the Hardy Boys clambered into the rickety Ford and the two men resumed their seats in front.

"As soon as I saw that car on the road I knew it was the same car that ran down my chickens!" declared the driver. "And when I saw them fighting with you boys, I knew they weren't up to any good and I knew what side I was going to take. And I took it!"

"Yes, sir, we sure sent them running!" His companion chuckled.

"A mighty good thing for us that you showed up when you did," Frank declared. "That gang were trying to kidnap us."

"How come?"

"They've been trying to keep us from catching a train to the West, and they mighty nearly got away with it that time."

"Well, they won't harm you again—not as long as you're in this automobile," the big farmer assured them.

As the car bounded along onto the main highway, the Hardy boys discussed the trap into which they had been so cleverly led.

"It'll teach us to beware of strangers from now in," Frank said. "Evidently one lesson isn't enough."

"If a stranger says so much as 'Hello' to me after this I'll yell for the police."

"Perhaps not that bad," and Frank grinned. "But we know now that there is a plot on foot to keep us from reaching the West, and we'll have to be on our guard."

"I'm more anxious than ever to get to the West now. It looks as if we're heading into some real excitement."

"We've had more than we bargained for already."

In a short time the automobile came within sight of the town the boys had left but a little while before, and after warmly thanking their two rescuers and slipping a five-dollar bill into the hands of the big driver, who beamed with gratification and delight, the Hardy boys settled down to wait for the night train back to Chicago. They were bothered by no more encounters with strangers, and after an almost interminable wait the train arrived.

"One day lost on our journey," remarked Frank, as the train pulled away from the station and headed northward.

"It could have been worse. If those fellows had captured us we'd have likely been held prisoners in some out-of-the-way place for ever so long."

"That's true, too. Well, we won't take any more chances. When we get to Chicago we'd better change our names and our appearance too, if we can manage it. If these chaps are on the lookout for us they won't stop now that we've escaped from them twice. We can't be too careful.''

Joe agreed that his brother's idea was a good one, and for the rest of the tedious journey back to Chicago they whiled away the time by discussing ways and means whereby they might journey to the West without being identified readily as the Hardy boys by the mysterious enemies who seemed determined to prevent them from joining their father.

CHAPTER X

On Guard

Back in Chicago, the Hardy boys went to a hotel. They were careful not to go to the place at which they had stayed on their first arrival.

"Hopkins has likely been told of our escape by now and he may be on the lookout for us," said Frank. "We'll just stay under cover."

"That should be easy enough in a big city like Chicago."

"It's not so easy if they know where to look for you, and I don't think they'll give up yet. For some reason, they're evidently mighty anxious to keep us from getting out to Montana."

In their hotel room that night they discussed the problem of changing their appearance. They had already changed their names, registering as Charles Norton and William Hill of Cleveland, Ohio, in case some prowling member of the gang that had evidently been assigned to see that they did not reach Montana should happen to drop into the hotel and glance over the register.

"I think," said Frank, "that the very simplest way for us to disguise ourselves would be to wear spectacles. If they chance to be looking for us they'll never think of looking for two boys wearing glasses."

"Good idea!" approved Joe. "Let's go out and get them now."

"Too late now. Shops will all be closed. We'll get them in the morning."

They left the hotel early and found a shop near by where Frank was fitted with a pair of horn-rimmed glasses that gave him a studious and benevolent expression. Joe bought a pair of cheap spectacles with plain rims. The transformation was remarkable. Instead of a pair of merry, bright-eyed lads, one saw two solemn, near-sighted boys who looked for all the world as though they had never had an unrestrained boyish impulse in all their lives.

"By all rights we ought to carry some books under our arms, too," Joe suggested.

So, to make the transformation complete, they stopped at a bookstore and purchased two weighty volumes. And, when it came time for them to catch their train, no one would have recognized in the two, sad-faced, bespectacled, earnest young students, the irrepressible Hardy boys of Bayport.

To allay suspicion, they decided to board the train separately. Frank went first, while Joe remained in the concourse of the station for a few minutes. Then he followed.

It was just as well that they did this. Near the gate leading to their train loitered a tall, sharp-featured youth who scrutinized every one who passed. He gave Frank but a fleeting glance as he went by and when Joe passed him later his gaze merely rested casually on the boy for a moment.

Had the Hardy boys but known it, the sharp-featured youth had been deputed by the mysterious Hopkins to report if the Hardy boys should attempt to leave Chicago. However, his instructions had been to keep on the lookout for two boys, aged sixteen and fifteen respectively, one dark, the other fair, who would board the train together. So the bespectacled students who had boarded the train separately did not arouse his suspicion and after the train pulled out he reported to Hopkins that the Hardy boys were certainly not on it.

Having left Chicago behind them at last and being assured that they were this time on the right train, Frank and Joe settled down to await with some little impatience their arrival in Lucky Bottom. The novelty of the cross-continent journey had worn off and the scenery had lost some of its earlier fascination. The unforeseen delay they had experienced left them all the more eager to join their father, and they wondered if he would worry because of their failure to arrive in Lucky Bottom at the expected time.

Gradually the scenery changed. The countryside altered in contour. The landscape became rockier and more mountainous, and on the second day they found themselves entering Montana. A suppressed excitement seized them as they realized that before long they would be at the end of their journey.

"I wonder how dad came to be hurt," Joe said, after reading over their father's letter again.

"I've been thinking about that, myself," said his brother. "From what we've gone through, I'd judge that he has enemies working against him in this case he is working on."

"Do you think they may have shot him?"

"They might have disabled him in some way. He was able to write to us, anyway. There's that much to be thankful for."

The Hardy boys realized that if a gang were arrayed against them, as seemed only too evident from their experience in Chicago, they must be very much on their guard from now on, as they drew closer to their destination. This was forcibly impressed upon them by an incident that happened at a small station in the mountains, where the train stopped to take on water.

"I think I'll take a walk up and down the platform," remarked Frank. "Coming?"

Joe looked up from his book.

"No, thanks. I think I'll stay here and read."

Frank left the coach and strode slowly up and down the platform. It was only a small, weatherbeaten station and there were few people in evidence. The town consisted of only one street, and it was built at the base of a huge mountain. The snow came sweeping down from the great crags in shifting sheets.

A rough-looking man in fur hat and mackinaw lounged down the platform, then swung himself up into the train. He appeared to be looking for some one. When Frank saw him next he was descending from one of the coaches far ahead. He came back to the platform again and there he was joined by another man, a villainous looking fellow with a black beard.

"Did you see anything of them Hardy boys?" asked the bearded man in a low tone of voice.

Frank, who was standing close by, could not help but overhear. He was electrified by astonishment.

The man who had gone through the train shook his head.

"Nary a sign of 'em on that train," he said.

"I can't figure out what happened," said the bearded man. "They ain't been on any train that's passed through here—we're sure of that."

"This here is the only way they can get to Lucky Bottom. If they did manage to sneak out of Chicago we'd be sure to see 'em goin' through here."

"Mebby they didn't get out of Chicago. The boys there might have picked up their trail again and caught 'em."

"They would have wired us if they had."

"That's true, too." The bearded man scratched the back of his head in perplexity. "I can't figger it out at all. Well, it ain't *our* fault. We've done the best we could."

"Yeah, they can't blame us."

"You're sure you went all through the train?"

"Right through. There was no two boys on it. There was one lad sittin' in the Pullman readin' a book, but he wasn't like the description of either one of 'em. Wore glasses. Looked like he was a regular little willy-boy."

"Wore glasses, eh? Well, he wasn't one of the Hardy boys, then. They don't wear glasses."

The pair moved off down the platform.

"You'd better go through the night train

when it comes in. We'll keep on the lookout for 'em for a few days more until we get word one way or the other. The boss would be sore if they got through on us.''

"Well, they haven't got through yet. That's one thing certain." The two men moved out of earshot.

Frank was tingling with excitement. He stepped toward the train, intending to go to Joe and tell him what he had heard. Then he hesitated. The rough-looking man who had searched the train might conceivably think he had been mistaken and might go through the train again. If he saw the two lads together he might be suspicious, spectacles or no spectacles. So Frank sauntered unobtrusively up and down the platform until it was time for the train to leave. Then he swung himself on board, but not until the train was actually pulling out did he rejoin his brother.

"What kept you?" asked Joe, looking up.

Frank sat down and, in a low voice, recounted the incident of the platform. Joe listened in almost incredulous surprise.

"So it looks as though we've run the gauntlet at last," concluded Frank.

"Boy! it was certainly a bright thought of yours that we wear spectacles on this trip. He would have spotted me in a minute."

"It was luckier still that we weren't together

when he walked all through the train. If he had told that black-bearded man that there were two boys sitting together they might both have gone back for a second look at us."

"Well, we got out of it all right. I don't think there's anything more to be feared."

"Not until we reach Lucky Bottom."

"I wonder what we'll bump up against there."

"Plenty—by the looks of things so far."

The train continued on its laborious way through the mountains. It passed through little mining villages, abandoned camps, climbing on up to higher altitudes until, late in the afternoon, the Hardy boys heard the cry for which they had been waiting so long.

"Lucky Bottom! Lucky Bottom!"

CHAPTER XI

FENTON HARDY'S STORY

LUCKY BOTTOM was a particularly desolate place in the winter time. It was not especially prepossessing at any season, but when the cold winds blew down from the rocky mountainsides and when snow drifted deep in the narrow street Lucky Bottom seemed like a deserted village. It had once been a prosperous mining camp, but one by one the mines had been worked out until now there was but one left. A few prospectors made the village their head-quarters still, hanging on in the vain hope of some day making a lucky strike that would restore the town to its former grandeur, but the general impression prevailed that Lucky Bottom's days were numbered.

There were a few gaunt, hard-bitten indi-viduals on the station platform when the Hardy boys got off the train. They were the only passengers that day and evidently it was un-usual for any one to alight at Lucky Bottom, because the loungers stared at them as if they were beings from another world.

"Can you tell me where Hank Shale's cabin is?" asked Frank of one of the men leaning against the station.

The native shifted his chew of tobacco, spat into the snow, and reflected.

"Straight down Main Street," he said "Then you start climbin' the hill. When you get to the top of the hill you'll find Hank's place. You can see it from here."

He conducted them to the end of the platform and pointed to the top of a hill back of the collection of shacks comprising the town. The boys could see a small log cabin, almost hidden by trees and almost buried in the snow. The distance was not great, so Frank and Joe, after thanking the man who had directed them, started off toward the cabin.

They went through Lucky Bottom, which was nothing more than a collection of shacks and cabins ranged on either side of a wide street and struck out up the hill until the street came to an end. There they followed a narrow path through the snow until at length they reached Hank Shale's place.

Their approach had evidently been seen, because the door opened as they neared the cabin and an elderly man with heavy, drooping mustache stood awaiting them.

"You the Hardy lads?" he inquired, in a piping voice.

"Yes. This is Mr. Shale's place, isn't it?" returned Frank.

"Come in. Come in," invited Hank Shale, standing aside to let them enter. "We've been expecting you this last day."

The boys entered a small, two-roomed cabin, a typical bachelor's residence, which, however, was kept scrupulously neat. They had barely time to look around before Hank Shale led the way to the adjoining room.

"Your father's in here," he said. "Come along."

They followed the man into the bedroom, and there they saw Fenton Hardy lying on a small cot. He sat up in bed as they entered, and held out his hand.

"Hello, sons!" he greeted them, with his cheerful smile. "Glad to see you."

When greetings had been exchanged, Hank Shale took the boys' coats and hats and began setting the table for supper. Soon the cabin was redolent with the fragrant odor of coffee. While Hank was busy in the other room, the boys had a chance to talk with their father.

"But how did you get hurt, Dad?" asked Frank.

Fenton Hardy leaned back on his pillow with a sigh.

"I cracked two of my ribs," he told them.
"Tumbled down off a big rock back in the
mountains, and now I'm laid up until the ribs
mend again. I'm thankful it wasn't a great
deal worse."

"We thought perhaps some one had shot
you."

"No, it wasn't that bad. I was chasing a
fellow at the time, and if it hadn't been for
falling off the rock I would have caught him.
So my good friend Hank Shale insisted that I
come to his cabin until my ribs set again. It
isn't very serious, but it will keep me indoors
for a while. That's why I sent for you."

"You want us to take up the case where you
left off?"

Their father nodded.

"I'll be able to help you considerably, even
if I am laid up," he said. "But what delayed
you? We expected you here yesterday."

The Hardy boys glanced at one another.

"You must have enemies that knew we were
coming, Dad," Frank said. "They tried to
sidetrack us in Chicago. We were delayed a
whole day there."

"How was that?"

The boys then told their father of their meeting with the man who called himself Hopkins,
of being locked in the compartment on the
wrong train, of their fight on the road and of

their eventual return to Chicago. When they told him of their simple disguise on the trip westward he nodded approval. When they told him of the rough-looking man who had searched the train for them at the mining village he frowned.

"Just as I expected," he remarked. "Some one must have got their hands on a copy of that telegram I sent you."

"The operator wouldn't give it out."

"No. But they may have tapped the wires. They would know that if I sent a message it would be to bring some one out here to help me. And this gang I have been fighting are capable of anything."

"Who are they?"

"It's a long story, boys. But seeing that you're going to be working on the case, I may as well give you all the information I have. This case concerns a quantity of gold that was stolen from three miners. One of these men, called Bart Dawson—"

"Bart Dawson!" exclaimed Frank and Joe simultaneously.

Their father looked at them in surprise.

"Yes. Do you know him?"

"Why, that's the man Jadbury Wilson mentioned!" Frank exclaimed.

"And who, may I ask, is Jadbury Wilson?"

"We'll tell you later, Dad. It may not be

the same fellow, but he mentioned a miner named Bart Dawson. Go on with the story, and then we can tell you about Wilson.''

"Well, this chap Dawson called me out here on the case and told me that the gold was stolen from them by a gang of outlaws who have been terrorizing this district for years. The outlaws are known as Black Pepper's Gang.''

"Black Pepper! And his real name is Jack Pepperill.''

"You seem to know as much about these fellows as I do myself,'' said the detective, in surprise.

"We'll tell you how we happened to hear about him. It's the same man all right. Go ahead.''

"Black Pepper's gang stole the gold from these miners. I discovered that before I'd been working on the case two days. We laid a trap for two members of the gang and managed to capture them. Then we threatened them with imprisonment if they didn't tell where the gold had gone to. They declared that one member of the gang had deserted and had taken the gold with him. The gold was in four bags, and although the outlaws gave chase and finally caught this man, the bags had disappeared. Try as they might, they could not get the fellow to admit where he had hidden it. He denied the theft utterly, said he had seen nothing of the gold, and that night he escaped.

"The outlaws were of the opinion that the gold had been hidden somewhere in a deserted mine shaft. That was the story the two rascals told us, and it was while I was checking up on this story that I was attacked by Black Pepper himself. I managed to fight him off and disarmed him, but he got away so I chased him and it was while I was chasing him that I fell off the rock and cracked my ribs."

"And that's how the case stands now?"

"That's how it stands now. I don't know whether to believe the two outlaws we captured or not. They may have been telling the truth. The gold may have really been stolen by the chap who deserted them. They said he later escaped from them and that they thought he had probably gone back to where he had hidden the gold and made away with it."

"In that case there wouldn't be much chance of getting it again."

"It's that circumstance that makes me suspicious of the story. If the deserter had recovered the gold and cleared out, the outlaws would likely give up hunting for it and they would certainly give up bothering me. But they are still in the vicinity and I have an idea they know just where the gold is and are waiting for a chance to get their hands on it. I think this story about the chap deserting from the gang and making away with the loot is false. They just wanted to throw me off the trail and probably thought I'd give up the case and go back East, leaving them a clear field.''

''What is your theory about the gold?''

''I think they know where it is, all right. They have it hidden away safely but they don't dare remove it. They'll wait until the affair dies down and then they'll probably separate and leave this district, meeting somewhere else to divide the loot.''

''Our problem is—''

''To find that gold.'' Fenton Hardy looked steadily at his sons as he said this. ''I have a lot of confidence in you,'' he went on. ''It just requires a lot of hard work and keeping your eyes open. Mainly, it will keep the gang on the jump. They'll know we haven't given up the case and they'll be afraid to do anything. And now,'' he said, ''you might tell me how you happen to have heard the names of Bart Dawson and Black Pepper before.''

Frank and Joe then told their father of their meeting with Jadbury Wilson, the old miner who said he had once lived in Lucky Bottom. They deemed it best not to mention the fact that Jadbury Wilson suspected Bart Dawson of stealing from him. If Bart Dawson were

back in Lucky Bottom they felt safer in re-
serving this bit of information. They merely
told their father that Wilson had mentioned
the names of Dawson and Black Pepper, among
others, as having lived in Lucky Bottom at the
time he had been a miner there.

"What kind of chap is Dawson?" asked
Frank.

"One of the finest!" declared their father
promptly. "He is a real square-shooter, as
the miners would say. The loss of the gold
has broken him all up. He told me he had had
hard luck all his life and now that he had a
fortune within his grasp it was heart-breaking
to lose it again."

Frank could not help thinking that life had
evidently paid back Bart Dawson in his own
coin. He had stolen a fortune from Jadbury
Wilson after Wilson had endured hard luck for
years. Now he was getting a taste of his own
medicine. Still, it seemed strange that Fenton
Hardy should be so convinced of Dawson's hon-
esty if he were the type of man who would rob
his own partners.

"Come and get it!" piped Hank Shale, from
the next room.

"That's the supper call," laughed Mr.
Hardy. "You must be hungry after your
journey. Better go and eat. Hank will bring
me mine in here."

Nothing loath, the two boys went into the combination living room and kitchen, where Hank Shale was already dishing out piping hot beans and stew from an enormous pot. What with huge slabs of bread, thickly buttered, and excellent coffee, the boys sat down to their supper with a will. They ate off tin plates and drank from tin cups, but they agreed that no meal could have tasted better. Even the food of the dining car on the train, exquisitely cooked and served though it had been, seemed somehow to lack the flavor of this meal in Hank Shale's mountain cabin.

Hank, like most men who have lived a solitary existence, was a silent man. He said nothing throughout the meal, but as he watched the boys eat and as he responded to their request for second helpings, a slow smile crept over his wrinkled face.

"That's the best meal I ever ate!" declared Frank emphatically, when he had cleared his plate for the second time.

"Me too," agreed Joe.

"Glad ye like it," said Hank Shale, deeply pleased.

CHAPTER XII

The Cave-In

Next day, refreshed by their night's sleep, the Hardy boys set out on a systematic search for the hidden gold.

"There won't be much real detective work about this case," their father told them. "It will be just a plain case of plugging along and searching high and low for that gold. It is hidden somewhere, or the gang wouldn't be staying around. Hunt in all the abandoned mine diggings, in any place where it might possibly be hidden. You may follow that line or you may try to find where the outlaws are camping and possibly pick up some clues there."

With this to go on, Frank and Joe Hardy left the cabin in the morning. They decided to explore some of the abandoned diggings first.

"It's like hunting for a needle in a haystack," said Frank; "but we might have a bit of luck and stumble on the gold."

They did not go down into the town because

they knew that their presence in the camp would cause considerable talk and, although they had little doubt but that news of their arrival had reached the outlaws by now, they preferred to remain under cover as much as possible.

Hank Shale had suggested searching the workings of an old mine just over the brow of the hill, and toward this place they went. There was a faint trail through the rocks, although it had long since been snowed over, but the boys managed to find the workings without difficulty. They felt the exhilaration of the clear, cold air and the excitement of at last being at work on the mystery of the hidden gold.

The abandoned mine did not look very much like a mine. It was just a large pocket in the earth, with a shaft that sank down into the darkness. The shaft was but a few yards across and a rickety ladder led down into the hard rock.

"We may as well try this one for a start," suggested Frank. "We can easily tell if any one has been around recently."

They had brought electric flashlights with them, and without further ado Frank began to descend the ladder. Joe followed. Their descent into the abandoned mine was precarious. as at various places the rungs of the ladder were broken, but after descending about forty feet they came to the first and only level. The mine had evidently been a failure.

In the light of the flashlights they saw that they were in a rocky cavern about two hundred feet in length. Not a great deal of work had been done in the mine and it had evidently been abandoned years before. The boys found the cavern extremely cold and damp and they made haste to explore it.

When they had almost completed the circuit of the place, hunting carefully for any sign of recent removal of rock, for any place where the stolen gold might possibly have been hidden, they were of the unanimous opinion that no one had been in the place since it was originally deserted. There was not the vestige of a hiding place. The abandoned working was but one of many in that locality, one lucky strike in the neighborhood having sent other miners into a frenzy of excavation on their respective claims. It had been worked for a short time and then left to its fate.

"I don't think there's anything here," said Joe.

"I'm sure of it. Oh, well, we couldn't expect to find the gold right off the bat. There are lots of other mines to search yet, and most of them plenty deeper than this."

"Think we should go back?"

"Just a minute. There seems to be a passage here."

Frank's light had revealed a narrow opening at the extreme end of the cavern. He bent down and examined it more carefully.

"This seems to lead somewhere," he said. "I think I'll follow it." He crouched down and made his way on hands and knees into the passage. Joe waited until he had disappeared and then called after him.

"I'll wait here."

"If it leads anywhere I'll call you."

Joe could hear his brother scrambling along through the little corridor in the rocks. After a while the sounds died away. It was dark and lonely in the cavern in which he stood. He waited for Frank's summons to follow.

After five minutes there was still not a sound from the opening into which his brother had disappeared. Joe began to get anxious. He knelt down and flashed his light into the interior of the passage. There was no sign of Frank.

"I wonder if anything has happened to him," he muttered.

When another five minutes passed and there was still no sign of his brother, Joe decided to invade the passage himself. Anything might have happened. Frank might have been overcome by poisonous gases in the depth of the mine. He might have tumbled down some unseen pit and hurt himself. Flashing the light ahead of him, Joe crawled into the narrow corridor in the face of the rock.

For several yards the passage extended directly ahead; then there was a turning. Examining the corridor, Joe saw that it was not a natural opening in the rock, but had been constructed by human hands, for the marks of pick and shovel were plainly visible. It had been blasted out of the rock, and for a short distance the dimensions of the passage were of good size, but gradually they narrowed.

He had just gone past the turn in the tunnel when he heard a faint shout.

"Joe! Joe!"

It seemed to come from a long distance, and there was a note of appeal in it that told the boy his brother was in danger.

Scrambling on through the tunnel that seemed to open before him in the vivid circle of light, he made his way toward Frank. He heard the cry again, and this time it was louder. He shouted back:

"I'm coming. What's the matter?"

"I'm trapped here. My foot is caught."

On through the gloomy tunnel Joe went.

At last the light revealed the form of his brother some distance ahead. Frank was lying flat on the rocky floor of the passage, with his foot caught in a crevice between two heavy boulders. He had tried to climb over them, and one rock had evidently become dislodged, pinning his foot against the other.

"Are you hurt?" asked Joe anxiously, as he reached Frank's side.

"No. I'm all right. But I can't move my foot."

Joe put down the flashlight so that its glare clearly illuminated the scene. Then he went over to the boulder and exerted all his strength to move it. But the boulder was heavy. Had it struck Frank's foot directly it would have shattered it to a pulp. Fortunately, it had merely slid into position above the other rock, pressing against the boy's ankle and imprisoning his foot in the crevice between.

Frank was unable to lend his brother any assistance. He was lying face downward and was unable to rise to a sitting position.

"It's—mighty—heavy!" panted Joe, as he strove to move the heavy boulder. It refused to budge.

"Rest a bit and then try it again."

Joe sat down, breathing heavily.

"How did it happen?" he asked.

"I was crawling along through the tunnel when I saw this pile of boulders ahead. At first I was going to turn back, but I thought that when I had come this far it was foolish to turn around, so I started to climb over the boulders. Just as I was almost over, that big boulder slid down against the other one—and there I was. Lucky I didn't break my leg.''

"I'm afraid to move that boulder the wrong way, or it might roll over onto you. There's only one way to move it safely and that is to lift it straight up, just enough to release your foot. But I'm afraid I'm not strong enough.''

"Try it again, anyway.''

Again Joe applied himself to the heavy rock. Although he strained and gasped in his efforts to move it, the boulder defied his efforts and he was unable to budge it an inch. He made attempt after attempt, but it soon became evident that the effort was beyond his strength, and at last he was forced to sink back, exhausted, against the wall. He mopped his brow.

"Too heavy!" he declared, out of breath.

Frank was silent.

"If we only had a crowbar of some kind!" he suggested at last. "It wouldn't be hard to move it then.''

Joe looked up.

"Why, I saw a crowbar back in the mine!" he exclaimed. "It will be the very thing.''

"Go back and get it. You'll be able to move the boulder away without any trouble. Then we'll clear out of here.''

Joe picked up his flashlight and turned to retrace his steps into the main working of the mine.

"I'll only be a few minutes," he promised.

"Don't worry about me. I won't go away," said Frank, with a laugh. He could be cheerful even in the dangerous position in which he found himself.

Back down the narrow tunnel crawled Joe, back toward the cavern into which they had first descended. He remembered having seen a long iron bar lying at the foot of the shaft and he realized that it would be an ideal lever for moving away the boulder that imprisoned his brother. He made haste, not wishing to leave his brother too long imprisoned, and in a few minutes he was back in the great cave.

At first he could not find the iron bar, and he hunted about, flashing the light here and there into dark corners. At last he found it, near the foot of the shaft. It was quite heavy and one end of it lay beneath a heap of rocks.

Joe tugged at the iron bar.

At first it resisted his efforts. He put all his strength into the attempt and the bar slowly moved. A final tug and it came free so suddenly that he staggered backward.

It was this circumstance that saved his life.

For, in extricating the bar, he had dislodged the mass of rocks. With a rush and a roar they came tumbling down across the bottom of the shaft. Had Joe been standing beneath he would have been crushed to death.

Then, before the clattering had died away, came a sullen, hollow roar from higher up in the shaft. Timbers snapped and crackled. The old boards, long since rotting away, suddenly gave beneath the pressure of rocks and earth. An avalanche of stones descended into the shaft on top of the first downfall of rock. More, followed, showers of earth came rushing down and a cloud of dust pervaded the cavern.

Joe leaped back.

Then, with a roar like thunder, the entire shaft caved in. Rocks and timbers came tumbling down with a terrific crash. The air was filled with the noise of smashing timbers and falling rock. The faint light from the shaft that had given some vague illumination to the cave, was blotted out. The mine reverberated with echoes and shook with the force of the crash.

Silence reigned. It was broken by the sharp sounds of falling pebbles that descended in the wake of the avalanche. Then those noises too died away. The cavern was filled with a choking cloud of dust.

Joe was almost stupefied by horror. He realized to the full the peril of the situation.

"The shaft has caved in," he thought.

"We're trapped in the mine! We'll never get out alive!"

He turned his flashlight on the place where the shaft had been. The light revealed only a high, sloping hill of rocks and shattered timbers. The shaft was completely blocked. It would take an army of men to clear away the débris.

Joe realized that he and Frank would never be able to accomplish the task. And he knew there was no hope of assistance from outside, for no one knew where they were. It might be days before they were traced to the mine.

CHAPTER XIII

IN THE DEPTHS OF THE EARTH

JOE HARDY still had the iron bar in his hand. He had not relinquished his grip on it.

"That's what caused all the trouble," he said to himself. The sight of the bar reminded him of Frank, still imprisoned back in the tunnel. He knew Frank would have heard the crash and would be wondering what had happened.

"I may as well set him free first and then we can reason out what we are going to do."

He turned and, dragging the heavy bar behind him, made his way to the opening of the tunnel. When he reached it he crouched down and proceeded into the passage.

With the flashlight illuminating the way, he went on toward the place where his brother was imprisoned. He found that the collapse of the shaft had shaken the entire mine. Bits of rock and heaps of earth and dirt along the floor of the tunnel testified to the shock of the cave-in. But when he came to the place where the tunnel turned to the right, he found, to his surprise, that the turning had vanished.

Instead, there was a solid wall of rocks and boulders ahead of him!

At first, Joe could not believe his eyes. Then realization dawned on him. The collapse of the shaft had shaken loose the boulders and rocks that lined the tunnel at this point and they had fallen down to block the passage.

He stared incredulously at the rocky wall ahead of him. He was cut off completely from his brother. Then he shouted:

"Frank!"

There was no answer. His shout echoed and re-echoed in the narrow space of the tunnel.

He shouted again and again, but the echoes were his only answers. Once he thought he heard a faint cry from beyond the wall, but he could not be sure. Communication had been cut off. He realized that his peril was doubled now. With the shaft blocked, with the passage-way blocked, he was imprisoned underground in a small space, where the air would soon become foul and where suffocation would eventually end his life. He set his flashlight on the floor of the tunnel, seized the iron bar, and set to work to remove the blockade.

The task seemed hopeless. The rocks were piled up deeply and were so large and so tightly jammed together that it seemed impossible to remove them. Joe knew that if the roof of the tunnel had completely fallen in there would be little hope, as rock would continue to fall as fast as he removed the rock from underneath.

He pried away a huge boulder at the top of the heap and stood to one side as he exerted all the leverage of the iron bar. The great rock wavered, then rolled down the side of the heap into the open tunnel. Joe waited anxiously.

To his relief there was no crash of rock from the top of the tunnel. The removal of the boulder had left a small opening.

He shouted again:

"Frank! can you hear me?"

A surge of gladness passed over him when he heard his brother's voice in reply:

"I hear you. What's happened?"

"The shaft caved in."

"The main shaft?"

"Yes."

"I heard the crash. I shouted to you but I didn't hear any answer. Are you hurt?"

"No. I'm all right. I jumped back just in time."

"Where are you now? Can't you reach me?"

"The tunnel caved in, too. I'm trying to dig my way through to you."

There was a moment of silence. Clearly, the news came as a surprise to Frank.

"That's bad," he said, at last. "Do you think you can get through?"

"I think so. I have the crowbar with me." Joe attacked another rock on the heap, edging the end of the crowbar into a crevice.

"How bad is the cave-in?"

"Very bad. The whole shaft went."

"That means we'll not be able to get out of here."

"We may find a way."

"Well, try to get through to me first. Then we'll see what we're to do."

Joe continued his labors at the rock pile. One by one he managed to dislodge heavy rocks and boulders until at last he had cleared away an aperture of sufficient extent to admit the passage of his body. He shoved the crowbar ahead of him and crawled over the remaining rocks.

Within a few minutes he had reached his brother, who was lying in the same position in which Joe had last seen him.

"How's the foot?"

"All right," Frank answered. "It isn't hurting any. See what you can do with that crowbar."

Joe inserted the end of the crowbar beneath the boulder, resting the middle of the bar on the boulder beneath. Then, exerting all his strength, he weighed down on the bar.

Slowly, gradually, the great rock began to move.

"It's giving way!" cried Frank. "Just a little more—a little more!"

By means of the bar and the principles of leverage Joe was able to apply much more strength to the removal of the boulder than if he had tried to move it with his bare hands. He shifted his grasp, bore down on the bar again, and the great boulder rose higher.

"Good," declared Frank, dragging himself forward. "I'm free."

He extricated his foot from the crevice and Joe lessened his weight on the bar. The boulder fell back into place again. But Frank was no longer a prisoner.

"That's that!" Frank ejaculated, scrambling to a sitting position and beginning to rub his ankle to restore circulation. "I'm out of that little jam, anyway, thanks to you and that crowbar."

Joe sat down on a near-by rock.

"We're up against a worse dilemma now," he said.

Frank looked grave.

"I know it. Still, there may be a way out. You say there's no use trying to get back up the shaft?"

"None at all. The whole place caved in with a crash."

"What caused it?"

"That crowbar had evidently been left there to prop up a weak place in the side of the shaft, and when I moved it, the whole thing gave way. Some of the rocks came tumbling out, and then the side of the shaft caved in. If I hadn't jumped back in the nick of time *my* goose would have been cooked. There must be a couple of tons of rock in the shaft now."

"We couldn't dig our way through?"

Joe shook his head. "We'd be wasting time trying. I guess the only thing we can hope for is that somebody heard the crash and comes to see what happened."

"But they don't know we're down here."

"That's true, too. And they won't be very likely to start clearing away the shaft unless they know we're here. This mine was abandoned a long time ago, by the looks of things."

"They might see our footprints up to the side of the shaft."

"It was snowing when we came here. They may be covered over by now."

The boys were silent. They realized that their plight was almost hopeless. In the cold, dark depths of the earth, with their air supply cut off, they were facing suffocation, exposure and starvation, and there seemed not the slightest possibility of escape.

"The only thing to do," said Frank, at last, "is to keep on following this tunnel. There's no use going back into the mine itself."

"No, there's no use going back. But to my mind I don't think there's any use going ahead, either. This tunnel probably ends in a blank wall."

"We might as well find out. We won't do ourselves any good by just sitting here and waiting to die." Frank got to his feet and picked up his flashlight. "Better turn out your light," he advised. "We need only one light at a time and we might as well be saving the batteries."

Joe got up and did as his brother had suggested.

Frank went on down the passage, followed by Joe. The boys felt in their hearts that there was very little hope that the passage would lead anywhere, but it seemed to be the only possible avenue of escape. They recognized that it was only a "drift" that the miners had dug and blasted away from the main workings in an effort to discover a vein of gold, and the fact that it had not been further developed seemed to indicate that the search had been unsuccessful and that the drift had been abandoned.

"I wish we had told dad exactly where we were going to go to-day," said Frank as they went slowly on down the tunnel.

"So do I. There'd be a chance for us then. They'd send some one out to look for us, and then they could start to work clearing away that shaft."

"Well, we can be thankful we weren't in the shaft when it collapsed."

"Yes, it could have been worse. If I had been caught in the cave-in you would be lying under that boulder yet."

"We still have a chance as long as we have that crowbar and can keep moving." Frank paused. "By the way, do you feel a draft?"

"Seems to me I *do* feel cold air!"

"Perhaps there is an opening to this tunnel This seems promising."

The rush of cold air about their heads was soon quite evident. The boys' spirits rose forthwith and they proceeded through the tunnel more cheerfully.

"If air can get into this place we should be able to get out of it," said Frank. "Perhaps this tunnel is just another entrance to the mine."

"Let's hope so."

They continued, Frank flashing the light before him. The tunnel began to grow narrower. They had to crouch almost double in order to avoid bumping their heads on the rocky roof.

"Another minute or so and we'll know whether this place has an opening or not," called back Frank.

"It *must* have an opening! Where would that fresh air we feel be coming from if it hadn't one?"

"It might be coming through a small slit in the rocks. We can't depend on it too much. Ah! Here we are!"

His light had disclosed the fact that they were at the end of the tunnel. But his tones immediately changed to a murmur of disappointment when he saw that the tunnel ended in a sheer wall of cold, wet rock.

The boys crouched in silence gazing at the rock wall that seemed to crush all their hopes. The wall was a barrier that cut them off from all chance of reaching the sun-lit, outside world again.

"It's a blind alley!" said Joe, in a hushed voice.

Frank merely nodded. He had been buoying up his hopes by refusing to admit to himself that the tunnel could be anything else than an outlet to the mine. Now he was overwhelmed by disappointment.

"We're up against it," he said at last. "This tunnel leads nowhere and the shaft is blocked."

"I'm afraid so."

Joe tapped the crowbar tentatively against the wall of rock. It thudded dully. There was no hollow sound that might indicate another tunnel beyond. The dull ring of the iron bar seemed to sound their death-knell.

"I guess this is our finish, Frank," he said gravely.

CHAPTER XIV

ATTACKED BY THE OUTLAWS

THE Hardy boys were so profoundly discouraged by the discovery that the tunnel, their
sole hope of safety, ended in nothing but a
blank wall of rock, that for a while they sat
in the gloom, scarcely speaking. Their plight
was perilous and there seemed not the slightest
ray of hope.

At last Frank bestirred himself.

"I'm still thinking of that gust of fresh air
we felt farther back in the tunnel!" he said.

"There is fresh air coming in somewhere.
The air in here isn't getting foul."

"Let's go back and explore the tunnel again.
We might find an opening of some kind.

"It won't be big enough for us to get
through," predicted Joe, gloomily.

"Well, we'll go and see, anyway."

The boys turned back. Frank took the lead
again and they moved on. The flashlight cast
its bright circle of illumination on the dank
rock walls of their prison as Frank explored

every inch of the sides of the tunnel. For a while their scrutiny met with no reward. The tunnel was unbroken by crevice or cranny.

"We must have passed the place by now," said Joe.

"I don't think so. We'll keep on trying."

At last Frank gave an exclamation of satisfaction. He had felt a sudden rush of cold air against his face. It seemed to come from above and he stopped, flashing the light hither and thither.

"It's around here somewhere."

"I can feel the draft. There must be a big opening."

The circle of light ceased wavering and rested finally on a place at the side of the tunnel, toward the roof. It was just a dark patch, an indentation in the rock, but it was quite large and it seemed to indicate an opening of some kind. It was about five feet from the ground.

"I'll hold the light," Frank said. "See if you can clamber up and investigate that place, Joe."

He stepped back and directed the flashlight so that Joe was able to find a convenient foothold. Joe reached up and secured a grasp on the edge of the natural shelf of rock. Then he managed to scramble up the wall until he swung himself over the ledge. Frank stepped back farther and the light plainly revealed his brother kneeling on the rocky shelf.

"Find anything?" he asked.

"There's a powerful draft of air coming down through here," said Joe, in tones of suppressed excitement. "I think this is a sort of tunnel or air shaft through the rock. I'll turn on my own flashlight."

In a moment Frank could see the glow of his brother's light reflected from the rocks above. Then he heard Joe give a lusty shout of delight.

"It leads on up!" he called. "It is a tunnel running at an angle, and I think it goes to the surface."

"Can you see any light?"

"No. Nothing. But I think it won't hurt to explore it. By the force of the cold air rushing down through here I think it must lead to the top."

"I'm coming up."

Joe disappeared up into the tunnel and Frank, putting his flashlight into his pocket, scrambled up to the shelf of rock. There he knelt and turned on the light again.

He could see Joe ahead of him, crawling on up through the narrow passage. The tunnel in the rock was just as Joe had described it, a long, narrow shaft that led upward at a steep slope. It was not so steep that they would not be able to clamber on up to wherever it might lead.

"Go ahead," he called out. "I'll follow you."

"I hope it doesn't get narrower up ahead."

"We'll go as far as the tunnel lets us."

The two boys began crawling up the rocky shaft. Joe called back:

"It's widening out!"

And, truly, the shaft became gradually wider until the boys could almost stand upright in it. The draft of cold air blew against them with great force and roared and whistled down the tunnel. Suddenly Joe stopped and waved the flashlight back and forth.

"There's a drop here."

Frank joined him. There was room enough now for them to stand side by side, and the wavering flashlights showed them that they stood at the end of the tunnel and that it opened into a chamber of rock similar to the mine working they had first entered.

"Look, Joe! I think I see a glow of light away over there. Turn off your flash."

The flashlights were switched off and the brothers stood in total darkness. When their eyes became accustomed to the absence of the electric glow, they saw that almost directly across from them was a faint, bluish grey reflection of light.

"We've found our way into another mine," said Frank. "That must be the light from the shaft. There's a chance for us yet."

He switched on his light again and flashed it into the rocky chamber into which the tunnel led. They found that they stood but a few feet above the floor of the mine working, so they promptly leaped down and then began a cautious walk across the cavern. The floor was rough and strewn with chipped masses of rock which showed that mining had once gone on there, and once they stumbled over a pick that some one had left behind when the working was abandoned.

They drew closer to the light that emanated from the shaft, and at last their flashlights revealed a crude ladder leading up the wall. Here they were met by another rush of cold air. The draft created by the tunnel leading into the other mine was severe and the wind whistled about the cavern. At the bottom of the shaft the Hardy boys looked up.

The ladder led up a distance of about twenty feet, and they could see the blue sky above. The sight made them sigh with relief. It was as if a heavy weight had been lifted from them.

"Up you go," said Frank. "We'll be out of here in no time, now."

"I'll say we're lucky."

"I never thought we'd see daylight again.

The old sky looks pretty good, doesn't it?"

"Never looked so good to me before."

Joe put his foot on the first rung of the ladder. Although the mine had evidently been deserted many years before, the ladder leading down into the shaft still held firm. Slowly he began to ascend.

Frank came behind. Each was filled with relief that they had escaped imprisonment in the abandoned mine, imprisonment that might easily have meant a wretched death. The cold wind about their faces was like the breath of life to them.

Suddenly Joe stopped.

"Listen!" he whispered.

They remained still. Then, from above, at the top of the shaft, they could hear voices.

"That cave-in must have finished them," some one was saying. "The whole shaft is gone."

"They might have found their way out," replied another voice. "These two mines lead into each other."

"I didn't know that."

"Yes—there's a tunnel leading down into their main drift."

"Oh, those kids would never find it. Probably they were crushed to death by the cave-in, anyway."

The voices died away as the men evidently

moved back from the neighborhood of the shaft-head.

"Some one has been looking for us," said Joe, in a low voice.

"They've given us up for dead. They'll get a surprise when we pop up out of the ground. Evidently they weren't going to try to dig us out. Go on up."

Joe resumed his climb and in a few minutes he emerged above ground, stepping off the top of the ladder to a rickety platform covered with snow. Frank scrambled up beside him, and then the two brothers stared in amazement at what they saw.

Three rough-looking men were standing only a few yards away. One was a tall, surly chap in a short, fur coat. He was badly in need of a shave and his brutal chin and heavy jowls were black with a stubble of beard. The other two were short and husky of build. One was clean-shaven and thin-featured, the other had a reddish mustache. About the waist of one of the men, the thin-featured fellow, was a belt with a holster from which projected the butt of a revolver. The three were villainous in appearance.

As though some sixth sense warned the men that they were observed, they whirled about and confronted the Hardy boys.

The men were as surprised as the lads. Both

Frank and Joe realized that there was something unsavory about the strange trio and when they saw the thin-featured man suddenly reach for his revolver they knew that they were confronting not friends, but enemies.

"That's them!" shouted the man in the fur coat excitedly. "Grab them!" And with that he began to run toward the two boys. "No shooting!" he shouted to the thin-featured fellow, who promptly shoved his revolver back into the holster.

"Run for it," muttered Frank.

He wheeled about and commenced to run down the hillside in the general direction of the town.

The snow was deep and it hampered their movements, but the pursuers also experienced this handicap. Frank and Joe were exhausted by their gruelling experience in the mine and they were unable to make good progress. The man in the fur coat came leaping after them, ploughing through the snow recklessly. He gained rapidly on them.

"Stop or we'll shoot," he roared.

This was but a bluff, and the Hardy boys recognized it as such. They raced madly on through the deep snow that clung to their limbs and held them back. Joe was lagging behind, unable to keep up the pace. The man in the fur coat was only a few feet back of him. The fellow leaped ahead and sprang at Joe in a football tackle that brought the boy down. The pair went rolling over and over in the snow, kicking and scrambling.

Frank stopped and turned back. He could not desert his brother and he was prepared to be captured with him at the expense of his own freedom. He met the thin-faced man, who led the other pair of pursuers, with a slashing blow in the face that knocked the man off his balance so that he tumbled backward into the snow with a grunt of pain and amazement. The short, stocky man came on with a growl. Frank swung and missed; then his attacker closed with him and they struggled to and fro in the snowbank.

His assailant twined one foot about Frank's leg and they toppled over into the snow. By that time the thin man had scrambled to his feet and again launched himself into the struggle. Frank Hardy was completely overpowered.

He was dragged roughly to his feet, his arms gripped behind his back. Joe had been no match for his more powerful antagonist and he too had been forced to submit to capture.

The trio held the boys in their power.

"What'll we do with 'em?" asked the thin-faced man gruffly.

"Bring 'em back to the mine first," said the

fellow in the fur coat. "I guess the boss will want to see these birds."

Frank and Joe were roughly bundled up the hillside again by their captors. All the time Frank's mind was in a whirl. Who were these three men? Why had they attacked them? Why had they been hunting for them in the first place? And who was "the boss" they spoke of?

In due time they reached the shaft-head again and there the man in the fur coat faced them.

"Who are you two boys?" he demanded.

"Who are you?" countered Frank.

"That doesn't matter. What's your names?"

"Tell us yours first."

"What were you doing in that mine?"

"What did you attack us for? Why are you keeping us here?"

The man in the fur coat became impatient at receiving questions instead of answers.

"Are you the Hardy boys?" he asked. "Sons of that detective?"

"Try and find out."

"We'll find out, all right," declared the man in the fur coat threateningly. "We'll take you to somebody that'll make you talk."

"You'd better let us go or the whole three of you will find yourselves in jail," said Frank.

The man laughed shortly.

"No fear," he said. "Not in Lucky Bottom, at any rate." He turned to the other two men. "Keep these boys here," he ordered. "I'll be back in a while. Don't let them get away!"

"Where are you going, Jack?" asked the thin-faced man.

"I'm going to get Black Pepper. He'll make these birds talk."

With that the fellow stalked away through the snow. Frank and Joe glanced quickly at one another. They knew now the explanation of their capture. They were in the hands of three members of the gang of the notorious Black Pepper, the outlaw.

CHAPTER XV

THE TRAP

THE man of the thin features produced the revolver from its holster and sat down on a snow-covered rock near the top of the shaft. He held the weapon negligently, but there was no doubt that he could level it at the Hardy boys in a second if they attempted to escape.

"You can sit down if you want," he said. His partner still retained a tight grasp on Frank. "Let him go, Shorty. I've got this gun here and I guess they won't try to get away. We may as well be comfortable."

The fellow addressed as "Shorty" moved away from Frank and sat down by his companion. The Hardy boys found a heap of rocks near by and seated themselves. They knew there was no use of attempting to escape as long as that ugly-looking revolver was in the hand of their captor.

"Say, Slim," remarked Shorty, "do you think Black Pepper is at the camp?"

The other man nodded.

131

"Yeah! He came back this morning."

Slim looked up at the Hardy boys.

"What were you guys lookin' for in that mine, anyway?"

"Oysters," replied Frank, with a grin.

"None of your funny stuff," rapped out Slim. "We'll make you talk soon enough. We know what you're after."

"What did you ask us for, then?" asked Joe.

The outlaws were silent. They saw that nothing was to be gained by seeking information from the lads. They were content to await the return of Black Pepper and their companion Jack.

Frank and Joe Hardy sat on the snow-covered rocks in silence. Slowly Frank put his hand behind his back and began to grope about among the rocks. He knew that they were loose and that they were of various sizes. The idea had occurred to him that if he could but use one of them as a weapon he might be able to disarm Slim and perhaps effect his escape and that of his brother.

Bit by bit he groped about. One rock was too large for him to grasp. Another was too small to be of any use. Finally his hands closed about a good-sized stone that came from the rest of the pile without much difficulty.

He calculated the distance and eyed the revolver warily. Frank had been pitcher on the Bayport high school nine and the accuracy of his aim had often been the despair of opposing batsmen. Now he called on all his skill.

Without moving from his position he suddenly brought up the rock and flung it with all his strength directly at the revolver in Slim's hand. The outlaw's grip on the weapon had relaxed in his indifference, and when the stone struck its mark, full and true, the gun went flying into the deep snow.

"Come on, Joe!" shouted Frank scrambling to his feet. He had noticed a path leading through the snow in the direction of the road that went to Hank Shale's cabin and he ran toward this path with all the speed at his command. Joe had not been slow to grasp the situation, and he too came racing through the snow but a few paces behind.

The outlaws were taken off their guard. Slim instinctively reached for his rovolver, but it had disappeared in the snow and he wasted many precious seconds hunting for it. Shorty had leaped after the boys, then, seeing that his companion did not follow, he hesitated, ran back, and then turned around again. He did not know what to do.

"After them!" roared Slim, and Shorty took up the pursuit. But his indecision had given the Hardy boys the opportunity they needed. They had a good start on their pursuer and Shorty was but a clumsy runner at best. Frank gained the path and there his progress was swifter because he was not handicapped by the impeding snow. Slim finally abandoned his search for the weapon and also took up the chase, but by this time he was far behind.

The boys gained the main road, with Shorty ploughing along in pursuit. Even yet they were not safe, but chance came to their aid in the shape of a stage that ran from Lucky Bottom to one of the neighboring camps. It rattled along, with sleighbells jingling, the driver muffled to the ears, and when Shorty and Slim caught sight of it they slowed up and abandoned the chase. The open road was a dangerous place. They did not wish any interference from the stage driver or his passengers.

When Frank and Joe saw that their pursuers had turned back they slowed down to a walk. Hank Shale's cabin was already in sight.

"We gave them the slip, all right," declared Frank jubilantly.

"I'll tell the world we did. Black Pepper and the other fellow will be hopping mad when they come back and find that we've escaped."

"We'll have to be on the lookout for them

from now on. They won't stop until they do lay their hands on us."

"Perhaps it's just as well. We can be on our guard. If we weren't expecting anything wrong we'd be liable to walk right into their arms."

When the boys reached the cabin they found their father and Hank Shale greatly worried by their prolonged absence. They told of their descent into the abandoned mine, of the cave-in, and of their subsequent escape, of their capture by Black Pepper's men and of their getaway. Mr. Hardy looked grave.

"I think we'd better drop the case," he said finally. "It's too big a risk to take."

"Why?" asked the boys, in surprise.

"You might have been buried alive in that mine, in the first place. I would never have forgiven myself. And now that you have run up against Black Pepper's gang they'll be out to get you. I don't want to be responsible for making you run those risks."

"We won't drop the case," laughed Frank. "It's just getting interesting now. We'll find that gold for you, Dad."

"Don't worry about us," chimed in Joe. "We can look after ourselves. We probably won't be up against any worse dangers than the ones we faced to-day."

"Well" said Mr. Hardy, reluctantly.

"you've come all the way out here, and I suppose you'll be disappointed if I don't let you go ahead; but I don't want you to take any unnecessary risks."

"I'm thinkin' they'll pull through all right," said Hank Shale solemnly. "Let the lads be, Mr. Hardy."

So, with this encouragement, Mr. Hardy consented to let his sons continue their activities on the case. Both Frank and Joe promised to take all due precautions and next morning they resumed their search for the missing gold.

During the days that followed they explored several abandoned workings, but the hunt was fruitless. They succeeded only in getting themselves well covered with dirt and grime and would return to the cabin hungry and weary. There had been no sign of any members of Black Pepper's gang. But finally Hank Shale, who had been down to the general store at Lucky Bottom one day, had news for them.

"They be sayin' down town," declared the old miner, "that Black Pepper and his gang have broke up camp."

"Have they left Lucky Bottom?" asked Mr. Hardy quickly.

Hank Shale shook his head. "Nobody knows. They had a camp somewheres back in the mountain, but they've all cleared away from it. Maybe the two lads here scared 'em."

"They've likely just moved to a new camping place," remarked Frank.

"I hope so," said Mr. Hardy. "If they've gone away it means that the gold has gone with them. If they're still around we have a chance yet."

Frank and Joe said nothing, but when they went to bed that night they talked in whispers in the darkness.

"What's the program for to-morrow?" asked Joe.

"We're going to find out if any of that gang are still around."

"Do you mean we'll go out looking for them?"

"Sure! It's just as dad says—if they've gone away the gold has gone with them. If they're still hanging around we'll know there's still a good chance of finding it ourselves."

"Where shall we look?"

"Up in the mountains. We can look around for trails in the snow."

"Suits me, as long as they don't catch us."

"That's a chance we have to take."

So next morning, without revealing their plans to any one, the boys started out into the mountains. It was a gloomy day and the sky was overcast. The lowering, snow-covered crags loomed high above them as they headed toward a narrow defile not far from the abandoned mine where they had been captured by Black Pepper's men some days previous. I was toward this defile that the man called Jack had gone on his way to summon Black Pepper, and the boys judged that the outlaws' abandoned camp was probably somewhere in that direction.

They discovered a narrow trail through the snow. It was a trail that had evidently been much used, for the snow was packed hard by the tramp of many feet.

"I think we're on the right track, all right," said Frank. "Even if we only find the deserted camp we may get some clues that will help us."

The boys went higher up into the mountain and at last they came to a protected spot beneath an overhanging crag, where the snow had not penetrated. Here the trail ended in a long platform of bare rock. They went across it, but were unable to pick up the trail again, although they searched about in every direction.

Suddenly Frank said to his brother in a low voice:

"Don't look around. Keep straight ahead."

"What's the matter?"

"There's some one following us. I just caught a glimpse of him out of the corner of my eye. He's hiding behind the rocks back there."

"Let's cackle him."

"There may be others with him. Let him follow, and if he's alone we'll grab him."

Without giving any indication that they had seen their pursuer, the Hardy boys cut down into a narrow ravine where huge masses of boulders made progress difficult. They came to a place where rocks rose on either side so close together that there was room for only one person to pass at a time. As soon as they had gone through the opening Frank leaped to one side, motioning to his brother to take the opposite side of the boulders. They were now completely hidden from the man who followed.

"We'll get him when he comes through," whispered Frank.

They waited expectantly.

At last they heard the crunch of snow that indicated the unsuspecting man was approaching. Cautiously he drew nearer, step by step. The boys prepared themselves.

The man drew nearer. He was just entering the passage between the boulders. Frank and Joe pressed themselves against the rocks. They saw a head appear in view, then the shoulders of the man. He stepped forward and, at the same moment, they sprang at him.

Frank launched himself full on the fellow's shoulders and he gave a cry of surprise. At the same time Joe flung his arms about the man's waist and all three came tumbling to the ground. There was a flurry of snow as they struggled, but the fight was short-lived. Taken completely by surprise, the man was quickly overcome. He had reached for a revolver at his waist, but Frank had seen it in the nick of time and had struck it from his grasp. He seized the weapon himself and pressed the barrel of it to the fellow's temple.

"All right! All right!" he gasped. "I give in."

There was something familiar about the voice. The man turned his head about and they saw that it was the man known as Slim, the thin-faced fellow who had been among their captors several days before.

CHAPTER XVI

INFORMATION

"So IT's you!" said Frank.

"Just my luck," muttered the outlaw, in disgust. "I might have known better!"

Still leveling the revolver at Slim, Frank relinquished his grasp and stood back. Joe also withdrew. Slim, holding his hands above his head and keeping a wary eye on the weapon, got to a sitting position.

"This is luck," Frank remarked. "We hadn't expected to meet again so soon."

"If I'd had any brains I wouldn't have let myself step into a trap like this," growled Slim.

"What were you following us for?"

"What were you doing up here?"

"Trying to find you," said Joe cheerfully.

"Where's Shorty and Jack and Black Pepper?"

Something in the man's question made Frank think quickly. Was it possible that Slim had become separated from the rest of the gang?

"I suppose you know the camp's broken up?" he remarked.

A look of surprise leaped into Slim's face.

"No," he said, hoarsely. "I've been away. What happened? You don't mean to tell me——"

"We're telling you nothing."

"They caught the gang?" went on Slim.

"Wait until we take you down to Lucky Bottom. You'll find out all about it then," said Frank, evasively. If Slim thought the rest of the outlaws were captured he might be more disposed to talk.

"I might have known it," said Slim gloomily. "They were gettin' too careless. I told 'em a hundred times they'd be tripped up, especially after lettin' you two give us the slip."

"We might be able to make it easier for you," Frank suggested.

"How?"

"If you've got any information to give us we might be able to put in a word for you."

Slim looked at them steadily for a moment. Then he asked:

"What kind of information do you want?"

"You know what we're hunting for."

"The gold?"

"Of course."

Slim was silent for a moment.

"That gang has been tryin' to double-cross me all along," he said at last. "I don't owe 'em nothin'. They would have cleared out with the gold and left me here if they could."

"Did they know where it was hidden?" asked Joe.

"Of course some one knew. They didn't dare make a get-away with it as long as Fenton Hardy was watchin' them. I guess the game is all up now, though. If they've got Black Pepper in jail they'll make him come through and tell where it was hidden."

"Don't the others know?"

Slim shook his head. "He wouldn't tell any of us. He hid the gold himself and we couldn't find out where. He said he was afraid we'd be double-crossin' him and stealin' it on him. I think he planned to take it himself and ditch the whole bunch of us."

"What do you know about it?"

"I know everythin' about it," said Slim boastfully. "Everythin' except where it was hidden."

"Who owned it in the first place?"

"You ought to know that as well as me. Bart Dawson and one of the Coulsons had it. Dawson blew into camp a while ago with Coulson and they dug up this gold. Dawson had it hid away some place. It must be about twenty years ago since he's been here. At

least that's what Black Pepper said. He was
in Lucky Bottom when Dawson was here before.''

The Hardy boys exchanged glances of surprise. The names of Bart Dawson and Coulson were familiar. These were Jadbury
Wilson's partners and the gold must be the
gold that Wilson presumed Dawson had stolen
from them. There was a mystery here that
they could not fathom. If Dawson had stolen
the gold, why did he bring Coulson back with
him? Why had he waited for twenty years before returning to dig up the loot?

''And Black Pepper's gang stole it from
Dawson?'' persisted Frank.

The outlaw nodded.

''Haven't you an idea where he hid it?''

''It was in one of the old mines somewhere
around here. That's how we knew you fellows
were after it when we found you were searching through the workings.''

''Where was your camp?''

Slim looked up at them. ''Don't you know?''

''We know it's deserted. We were on our
way to try to find it.''

''Don't kid me,'' sneered the outlaw. ''You
know where it is all right. You were headin'
right for it when I began to follow you. You're
not any too far away from it now.''

This was a stroke of luck that they had not

expected. Unwittingly, they had been on the right trail to the camp all the time.

"What are you going to do with me?" asked Slim.

"We're going to take you down to Lucky Bottom," said Frank.

"Aw, let me go," whined the outlaw. "I've told you all I know about it."

Frank shook his head.

"I think you'll be safer in behind the bars."

"The sheriff's a good friend of our gang. He'll fix things for me."

"That's up to you and the sheriff. If he tries to fix anything this time he'll get into trouble. We'll see to that. You'd better come with us."

Frank gestured with the revolver and Slim got unwillingly to his feet. Then, making the outlaw lead the way, the boys started back down the trail toward Lucky Bottom. Both Frank and Joe were anxious to resume the search for the outlaw's camp, but they were confident that they could find it now, from the fact that Slim had admitted they were on the right trail.

They made the journey back to town without incident. Their arrival, with Slim marching ahead and Frank keeping the outlaw covered with the revolver, created a sensation. Word quickly sped about the mining camp that one of

the members of Black Pepper's notorious gang
had been captured and a crowd congregated
about the jail as the little procession disappeared into the sheriff's office.

The sheriff was a shifty-eyed man of middle
age, obviously weak and susceptible to public
opinion. When he saw Slim led into the office
he scratched his head dubiously.

"We want this fellow locked up," said
Frank.

"What fer?" asked the sheriff reluctantly.

"For being mixed up in the gold robbery, for
one thing. If that isn't enough you can hold
him for carrying a revolver. If that isn't
enough we'll charge him with assault, pointing
a weapon, and half a dozen other things."

"I don't know," drawled the sheriff. "It
ain't quite usual——"

Clearly he did not wish to put Slim in a cell.
Frank became impatient.

"Look here," he said. "You're sheriff here
and your duty is to lock up lawbreakers. We'll
give you all the evidence you need against this
chap, but we want him kept where he can't do
any harm. If you're afraid of Black Pepper——"

"I'm not afraid of nobody," said the sheriff
hastily.

Just then the door opened and a bearded
old prospector strode in. He went right up to

the desk and shook his fist beneath the sheriff's nose.

"Lock him up" he roared. "We've stood for about enough from you, and I don't care whether you're sheriff or not. If you're goin' to encourage outlaws and thieves, me and the boys will mighty soon see that there's a new sheriff in this here man's town."

Frank and Joe then saw that other miners were standing in the doorway, crowding against one another, muttering truculently.

The sheriff blinked, wavered, and finally gave in.

"I just wanted to make sure it was all right," he muttered. "Don't want to lock anybody up that don't deserve it."

"You know mighty well that Slim Briggs deserves it, if any one in this camp ever did," retorted the old miner. "Lock him up."

The sheriff took a ponderous bunch of keys from his pocket and unlocked a heavy door leading to the cells. "This way, Slim," he said regretfully.

Slim Briggs followed him into the cell. He looked around, plainly expecting to see the rest of the gang in jail as well. Suspicion dawned on him.

"Where's the others?" he demanded wrathfully.

"What others?" asked the sheriff mildly.

"Black Pepper—the rest of the boys."

"They ain't here."

Slim gaped in astonishment.

"They ain't here?" he shouted finally. "Why, those boys told me they'd all been rounded up! I spilled everything I knew, just so I'd get let off easy!"

"You're the only one that's been pinched," said the sheriff.

"So far," added Frank pointedly.

Then, as Slim Briggs burst into a wild outbreak of bitter recrimination against the way in which he had deceived himself, the boys withdrew and the cell door clanged.

The old miner laughed and slapped Frank on the shoulder.

"I guess Bart Dawson come along just in time!" he declared. "Sheriff would have let that bird go if I hadn't got the boys to back you up." He turned to the sheriff. "We've seen that Slim is in jail," he said. "You're responsible for keepin' him there. If he gets out—" he snapped his fingers ominously— "it means a new sheriff in Lucky Bottom."

CHAPTER XVII

The Outlaw's Notebook

"Are you Bart Dawson? asked Frank.

"That's me," said the old man. "I'm the fellow they stole that there gold from."

The Hardy boys looked curiously at the old miner. From what they had heard of Bart Dawson from Jadbury Wilson they had been prepared to dislike him. But he appeared so genial and friendly and his grizzled old face was apparently so honest that they could not help but feel drawn to him. He certainly did not look like the sort of man who would desert his partners and rob them in the way Jadbury Wilson had described. Still, the evidence seemed all against him. He had betrayed his comrades and decamped with their gold, according to Wilson's story.

But why, argued Frank, should he wait twenty years to return for the wealth he had hidden? Why should he return with one of the Coulsons? Could it be possible that the pair had been in league with one another against Jadbury Wilson? The mystery defied explanation, but the more Frank looked at the jovial, honest face of the old man before him the more he was convinced that Bart Dawson had none of the earmarks of either thief or traitor.

"We've got one of 'em behind the bars now," said Dawson, rubbing his hands with satisfaction. "I only wish we had 'em all."

"Perhaps we will have them all before long," remarked Frank. "We've run across a few clues that may lead to something."

"That's good! That's good!" declared the old man. "Do your best, lads, and you may be sure Bart Dawson won't forget you."

Frank and Joe forbore any mention of the name of Jadbury Wilson. It was best, they decided, to keep that information to themselves until they should learn more about the affair of the stolen gold. They had long since learned that one of the axioms of successful detective work is to listen much and say little. Accordingly, they bade good-bye to Bart Dawson and left the jail.

"Where to?" asked Joe.

"Back to where we caught Slim Briggs. We were on the right trail to the camp."

"But if the outlaws have left there isn't much use going up there now."

"We never know what we'll find."

The boys made their way up into the mountains again and, after about an hour of steady traveling, found themselves on the trail that led into the defile where they had trapped Slim so neatly. On the way they discussed their meeting with Bart Dawson.

"I can't imagine that old fellow being the kind of man who would desert his partners and steal their gold, the way Jadbury Wilson described," said Frank, for the tenth time. "I just can't figure it out at all! You can tell with half an eye that he isn't a crook."

"Yet Jadbury Wilson was absolutely convinced that he had left them all in the lurch."

"And he had the gold in his possession. We know that. He came back here to dig it up. That shows he must have hidden it, as Wilson said he did. The whole story hangs together mighty well."

"Yet why should he bring Coulson with him?" objected Joe.

"That's another queer angle. I can't figure it out at all. I think we should see Coulson and tell him what we know, tell him what Jadbury Wilson told us, and ask him about it."

"That's the best idea. But isn't it strange how Jadbury Wilson, away back in Bayport, should be connected with this case, away out here in Montana?"

"It's a coincidence, all right. We just seem

to have blundered into the affair from both ends. Bart Dawson and Coulson know a lot that we don't know, but then we know a lot that Bart Dawson and Coulson don't know.''

"I think we hold the advantage. To-morrow we'll try to find Coulson.''

The boys were going down the defile now and they passed between the overhanging rocks where they had captured the outlaw. The marks of the struggle were still plainly evident in the snow.

"Poor Slim!'' remarked Frank, with a laugh. "He'll be kicking himself all around the cell for talking so much.''

"He was nicely fooled. He was sure the rest of the gang were all in jail.''

"We didn't tell any lies about it. He took it for granted that the outlaws were arrested. All we did was to look wise and let him keep on thinking so.'' The boys chuckled at the recollection of the ease with which the dull-witted Slim had been duped.

"If only the rest of them are that easy!'' said Frank.

"No such luck. I'm thinking this Black Pepper will give us trouble before we are through. He seems to have Lucky Bottom pretty well under his thumb.''

"He has the sheriff buffaloed, at any rate, by the looks of things. If Bart Dawson hadn't

shown up when he did I don't think Slim
Briggs would have been put in jail at all."

The trail now led toward a clump of trees,
and here there were evidences of recent habi-
tation. Some of the trees had been chopped
down, presumably for firewood, and the
stumps rose above the level of the snow.
There were numerous footprints about the
little grove and in some places the snow was
closely packed down. As the boys drew closer
they caught a glimpse of a small cabin in the
midst of the grove.

"We'll go easy from now on," said Frank
quietly. "Some of them may have come
back."

The boys went cautiously forward, keeping
to the shelter of the trees as much as possible.
Every few moments they would stop and listen.

But they heard not a sound. There was not
a voice from the cabin. The only noises were
the rustling of the trees in the wind. Quietly,
the Hardy boys stole up toward the cabin. It
stood in a little clearing in the wood. At the
edge of the clearing they waited, but still they
heard nothing, and finally Frank was satisfied
that the place was, in fact, deserted.

"No one here," he said, in a tone of relief. "We'll take a look around."

They advanced boldly across the clearing,

directly toward the door of the cabin. It was half open. Frank peered inside.

The place was deserted. The cabin was sparsely furnished, with a rude table, two chairs, and bunks on either side. There was a small iron stove at the far end of the building and the place was dimly lighted by one window.

There was every evidence that the outlaws had left the place in a hurry. Papers, articles of clothing and rubbish of all kinds lay about the floor, scattered here and there in abandon. One of the chairs was lying overturned on the floor. The place was in confusion.

The boys entered.

"Looks as if they didn't waste much time in getting out," remarked Joe.

"I'll say they didn't. The cabin looks as if a cyclone had hit it."

"Wonder if there'd be any use looking through those papers." Joe indicated a scattered heap of old envelopes, letters, tattered magazines and torn sheets of paper lying on the floor.

"That's just what I was thinking." Frank scooped up a handful of the papers and sat down on a bunk. He began to sort them over. The magazines he flung to one side as worthless. Some of the sheets of paper contained nothing but crude attempts at drawing or

penciled lists of figures presumably done by
some of the outlaws while idling away their
time in the cabin.

One or two of the letters, Frank put to one
side, as liable to give some clue to the identity
of members of the gang. When he had looked
through the first handful of papers he picked
up some more.

Suddenly he gave an exclamation of satisfaction.

"Find something?" asked Joe.

"This may be valuable." Frank held up a
small black notebook and began flipping the
pages. On the inside of the cover he read:

"Black Pepper—his book."

"This is the captain's own little record
book. There should be some information
here."

Frank began studying the book carefully.
The first few pages gave him little satisfaction, the writing consisting largely of cryptic
abbreviations evidently in an improvised code
known only to the outlaw himself. There
were the names of several men written on another page, and among them he recognized the
names of Slim, Shorty and Jack, the trio who
had captured them at the abandoned mine
working. Across from their names had been
marked various sums of money, evidently their
shares of the gang's takings in some robbery,

Then, on the next page, he found a crude map.

He studied it curiously. It looked something like the ground floor plan of an extremely crude house. There was one large chamber with two passages leading from it. One of these passages was marked with an X, and each passage led to a small chamber. From one of these led still another passage which branched into a tiny room, in one corner of which was inscribed a small circle.

"That's the funniest plan of a house I ever saw!" said Joe, looking over his brother's shoulder.

Frank studied the plan for a few moments and then looked up.

"Why, it isn't a house at all. It's a mine!" he declared. "This is the plan of a mine. This big room is the main working at the bottom of the shaft, and these passages are tunnels leading out of it."

"Perhaps it's the mine where the gold is hidden!" cried Joe, in excitement.

"There may be something about it on another page." Frank turned the leaf of the notebook. There he found what he was so eagerly seeking.

At the top of the page was written, in a scrawling, unformed hand: "Lone Tree Mine." Beneath that he found the following:

"Follow passage X to second cave, then down tunnel to blue room. Gold at circle."

Frank looked up at his brother.

"This is what we wanted," he said jubilantly. "They've had the gold hidden there all the time. All we have to do now is find the Lone Tree Mine and we'll recover the stuff in no time."

"Unless the outlaws have taken it away by now," pointed out Joe.

"That's right, too. I hadn't thought of that. They may have taken it away right after they abandoned this camp. Well, we've just got to take our chances on that. If they've left it in the mine this long they may think it's safe enough there a while longer." Frank got up from the bunk and stuffed the notebook into his pocket. His eyes were sparkling with excitement. "Joe, I believe we're on the right track! We know just where the stuff has been hidden and I've a hunch it's there yet. We haven't any time to lose. Let's start right now, before those rascals get ahead of us, and hunt for the Lone Tree Mine."

"Why, I'll bet I know where that is!" declared Joe. "Don't you remember an old mine working near where they caught us the other day? There was a big pine right by the top of the shaft, standing all by itself."

"I'll bet that's the place! Come on! We'll try it, anyway!"

Hastily, they left the little cabin. They were sure now that they were on the trail of the hidden gold. Frank remembered the lone pine tree that Joe had mentioned; it seemed to identify the abandoned working as the place they sought.

It was snowing heavily as they started down the trail but the boys scarcely noticed it in their excitement. They even forgot that they had not had their lunch.

"If the outlaws haven't beaten us to it," declared Frank, "we'll have that gold before the day is out!"

CHAPTER XVIII

The Blizzard

The Hardy boys set off down the trail at a good pace. The wind howled down from the crags and whistled through the trees. The entire mountain was veiled in a great mist of swirling snow and, as the wind rose, the snow stung their faces and slashed against them.

"Storm coming up," said Frank, burying his chin deeper into his coat collar.

"I hope it doesn't get any worse. We'll never find the place."

"We won't give up now. If we wait until to-morrow it may be too late."

The storm grew rapidly worse. The snowfall was so heavy that it obscured even the tops of the great masses of rock and it quickly drifted over the trail so that the boys were forced to follow the path by memory. This was difficult, as in some places the trail had wound about through tumbled masses of boulders and when it was hidden by snow they had to guess at its intricate windings. Several times Frank lost it altogether, but he was always able to pick up the trail again in some place that was sheltered from the storm.

The boys struggled on in silence. The wind was increasing in volume and the snow was so heavy that Joe could scarcely see the dim form of his brother but a few yards ahead. Suddenly he saw his brother stop.

"I've lost the trail!" shouted Frank, turning back.

They were standing ankle deep in snow. There was not the slightest vestige of a path. High above them they could discern the gloomy mass of a steep rock cliff and before them loomed a sloping declivity of rock that afforded not the slightest foothold.

"I lost the trail farther back, but I thought I was following it all right and could pick it up farther on. We'll have to turn back."

They retraced their steps. So furiously was it snowing that their own footprints were almost obliterated and they could scarcely find their way back to the place where they had left the trail. They found it again, however, and struck out in another direction.

It was growing bitterly cold, and although they were warmly clad they began to feel the effect of the chill wind that swept down from the icy mountain slopes. They pulled their caps down about their ears and made their

way slowly forward against the terrific wind
that buffeted them and flung sheets of snow
against them.

Frank gave a shout of triumph when he
finally picked up the trail again in the shelter
of some huge rocks where the snow had not
yet penetrated.   They advanced with new
courage.

At length they emerged through the defile
where the trail to the outlaw's deserted camp
led off the main trail up the mountain, and
then they rested.

Far below them they could see the slope of
the mountain, veiled in sweeping banners of
snow that shifted and swirled madly in the
blustering wind.   The town was hidden from
view, obscured by the white blizzard.

"Do you think we should try to make it?"
asked Frank.

"The mine?"

"Yes."

"You're leading this procession.   Whatever
you want to do."

"If you think the storm is too bad, we'll
start for the cabin."

"What would you rather do?"

"I hate to give up now, replied Frank, after
a moment of hesitation.

"I feel the same way about it," Joe said.
"I vote we try to find the mine.   Once we get

there we'll be able to get in out of the storm, anyway.''

"I thought you'd say that," laughed Frank. "We'll head for the Lone Tree Mine then. As far as I can remember it is just below us, and then over to the right.''

"We'll find it, I guess."

They started down the slope. But once they left the shelter of the rocks where they had rested they found that the fury of the storm was increased tenfold on the mountainside. The full force of the blizzard struck them.

The wind shrieked with a thousand voices. The snow came sweeping down on them as though lashed by invisible whips. The roar of the storm sounded in their ears and the fine snow almost blinded them.

"It's worse than I thought," muttered Frank.

The slope was steep and precipitous. They could not distinguish the details of the trail other than as a vaguely winding path that led steadily downward. Frank lost his footing on a slippery rock and went tumbling down the declivity for several yards before he came to a stop in a snowbank. He got to his feet slowly and limped on, suffering from a bruised ankle.

The trail wound about a steep cliff and he skirted the base of it, then disappeared between two high masses of rock. Joe could

dimly see the figure of his brother, and he hastened on so as not to lose sight of him.

But when Joe came around the rocks he was
confronted by an opaque cloud of snow, like a
huge white screen that had dropped from the
skies. He could not see Frank at all.

He followed the trail as well as he could, but
in a few moments he came to a stop. He was
out on the open mountainside and the winds
at this point converged so that the snow
seemed to be swirling about him from all sides.
The faint trail had been wholly obliterated.

He shouted.

"Frank! Frank!"

But the wind flung the words back into his
teeth. A feeling of panic seized him for a moment, but he quickly calmed himself, for he
realized that when Frank looked behind and
saw they were separated, he would retrace
his steps.

He went on uncertainly a few paces, until
it occurred to him that he might be wandering
in the wrong direction and that if Frank did
turn back he might not be able to find him.
So he tried to return to the trail again. But
the snow was falling so heavily by now that he
seemed to be wandering in an enormous grey
void, from which all direction had been erased.

He was hopelessly lost, so he stood where he
was and shouted again and again. There was

no answer. He could only hear the constant
howling of the wind, the sweep and swish of
snow.

Once he thought he heard a faint cry from
far ahead, but he could not be sure, and although he listened intently he could hear it no
more.

As he stood there on the rocks, with the
snow sweeping down on him and with the wind
howling about him, with only the gaunt,
gloomy shapes of the boulders looming out of
the heavy mist of storm, Joe felt the icy clutch
of the cold and he began to beat his arms
against his chest so as to keep warm. He
knew the danger of inaction in such a blizzard.

Anything was better than remaining where
he was. He struggled forward, slipped and
fell on the rocks, regained his feet, and moved
slowly on into the teeth of the wind. He did
not know whether he was following the trail
or not but, to the best of his judgment, he tried
to descend the slope.

As for Frank, he had been plunging doggedly on through the storm, confident that Joe
was close behind, and it was not until he had
gone far down the trail that he became aware
that his brother was not following. He turned,
and when he could no longer discern the figure
in the storm behind he retraced his steps
shouting at the top of his lungs.

There was no answer.

He searched about, going to left and right of the trail. He did not dare go far, being fearful of losing the trail himself. Frank was alarmed lest Joe had slipped and fallen on the rocks and injured himself. If he were unable to proceed he would freeze to death, lying help-less on the mountainside

With this thought in his mind, he searched frantically. He tried to follow back up the trail, but the snow had swept over his foot-steps and he soon found himself knee-deep in a heavy drift and he knew he had lost the path.

He tried to regain the trail, but the white screen of snow was like a shroud over the rocks and he had lost all sense of direction.

He floundered about in the snow aimlessly, but the trail constantly evaded him. Frank set his jaw grimly and went hither and thither, stopping every little while to shout. He knew that the wind drowned out his voice and he re-alized the futility of his cries, but still he hoped that there was just a chance that Joe might hear him.

Frank Hardy felt an overpowering sense of loneliness as he wandered about among the rocks and the deep drifts. He seemed to be alone in a world of swirling, shrieking winds and flailing snow that stormed down from a sky of leaden hue.

He shouted again and again, but to no avail. It was mid-afternoon, but the sky was so dark that it seemed almost dusk. If darkness fell and they were lost out on the mountain there was little hope that they would survive until morning. They would perish from exposure.

"I'd better go back to Hank Shale's place and get a searching party to come up and look for Joe," he thought.

This seemed the only sensible solution. But when he turned and tried to find the trail down the mountain again he found that it eluded him. There was not the vestige of a trail, not the sign of a path.

"And I'm lost too!" he muttered.

The wind shrieked down from the rocks. The snow swirled furiously about him. The blizzard raged. The roaring of the storm drummed in his ears as he stumbled and floundered about among the rocks and snow.

The Hardy boys were lost, separated, in the storm.

CHAPTER XIX

The Lone Tree

Suddenly, Frank Hardy had an inspiration. In the shelter of some rocks he cleared away the snow, then began to search about for wood in order to build a fire. If he were lost the best plan was to build a fire which would serve the double purpose of keeping him warm and possibly guiding Joe toward him as well.

He found some small shrubs and stunted trees and managed to break off enough branches to serve as the basis of a fair-sized blaze. He had matches in a waterproof box in his pocket, and after several unsuccessful attempts he finally managed to get a fire going. The wood was damp, but the small twigs caught the blaze and within a few minutes the flames were leaping higher and higher and casting warmth and radiance.

Frank crouched beneath the rocks and warmed himself by the fire. Once in a while he got up and went away to search for more wood to cast on the blaze. Occasionally he peered through the screen of snow in the hope of seeing some sign of Joe. At intervals, he shouted until he was hoarse in the hope of attracting his brother's attention.

The flames leaped up in the wind and as he piled more wood on the blaze the fire grew brighter. It was in a sheltered spot where the gusts of snow could not quench the flames.

At last he thought he heard a faint shout.

Frank sprang to his feet. He gazed through the shifting veil of snow that swirled about his shelter, but he could see nothing. Then he called out:

"Joe!"

The fire roared. The wind shrieked. Snow slashed against the rocks above him.

Then, out of the inferno of wind and snow he heard the shout again, and a moment later he caught sight of a dim figure plunging toward him. He ran forward.

It was Joe. He was almost exhausted and he was blue with cold. He staggered over toward the blaze and collapsed in a heap beside the fire.

"Thank goodness I saw the flames!" he gasped. "I was almost all in. I couldn't have gone another step."

"I thought I'd never find you. I hunted all over."

"I got lost. I couldn't find the trail."

"We're both lost now. I got off the trail myself when I was looking for you."

"I don't much care where we are so long as we're together again and we have a fire."

Joe extended his trembling hands to the blaze. In a short while he ceased shivering, and as the warmth pervaded his chilled body his spirits rose.

"That fire was a lucky thought," remarked Frank. "I was cold and it just occurred to me that you might see a fire through the storm even if you couldn't see me."

"I just caught a faint glimpse of it—just like a little pink patch shining through the snow. I was just about to give up and lie down on the rocks when I saw it."

"You'd have died of exposure."

For a while the two lads were silent as they thought of how narrowly the blizzard had been cheated of its victim. Then, when Joe had become warmed by the fire, they began to consider their course of action. Frank looked out at the storm.

"The wind seems to be dying down a bit," he said. "I can see farther down the mountain now than I could a while ago."

"Think we ought to start home?"

"Do you feel well enough now?"

Joe got to his feet.

"Sure. I feel fine now. There's no use

staying up here until nightfall. This storm may last a couple of days.''

''All right. Let's go.''

They stamped out the fire and resumed their journey down the mountain. They stayed close together this time, taking no chances on again being separated. As Frank had noticed, the wind had indeed lost much of its fury, although it still howled and blustered on the mountain slope, and the snow still fell steadily in a drifting cloud. The trail was almost obscured by the snowdrifts but Frank was able to find and follow it and they finally reached the place where they had turned off toward the abandoned mine workings several days before.

Here they hesitated.

''What do you think?'' Frank asked.

''Now that we're so close to the mine I think we may as well go on with our search.''

''I was hoping you'd say that. It shouldn't take us more than an hour or so and it isn't dark yet. Besides, we have our flashlights.''

''I haven't mine. But one's enough. Go ahead. It shouldn't be hard to find the Lone Tree from here.''

Frank turned off the trail. He headed directly toward the old mine workings they had previously visited and from which he remembered having seen the lone pine tree. The snow was deeper than they had expected and they ploughed through drifts up to the waist. They went on, however, and in a short while reached the abandoned mine of their harrowing experience underground. Here they paused.

"The lone tree was over to the right, I think," said Joe.

They peered through the storm. They could see nothing but drifting snow and the dull masses of the rocks. A shift in the wind raised the curtain of storm for a moment and then, like a gloomy sentinel, they saw the tall pine tree, solitary against the bleak background of grey.

"That's it!"

Now that their goal was definitely in sight they felt invigorated, and they hastened on through the snow toward the tree with new vitality. Forgotten for the moment was their weariness and exhaustion, the cold and the snow, in the lure of the gold that they felt sure lay somewhere in the neighborhood of that lonely tree.

Stumbling and plunging through the snow, they reached their goal at last. The tree creaked and swayed in the wind, and as they stood beneath it they saw that they were standing on the verge of a deep pit that seemed to have been scooped out of the earth by giant hands. There were a few ramshackle ruins of old mine buildings near by. The roofs had long since fallen in and the buildings sagged drunkenly. At the far side of the bottom of the pit, clearly discernible against the snow, they saw the wide mouth of a cave.

"That must be the shaft opening," said Frank. "We're on the track now."

The boys descended into the pit. The going was precarious, for the rocks were slippery and the snow concealed crevices and holes, so that they were obliged to proceed cautiously. But at length they reached the bottom and made their way across to the mouth of the cave.

Frank produced his flashlight as he prepared to enter.

"Stick close behind," he advised his brother. "We don't know what we're liable to run into here."

The snow flung itself upon them and the wind shrieked with renewed fury as they left the unsheltered pit and entered the half darkness of the cave mouth. It was as though they were entering a new world. They had become so accustomed to the roaring of the gale and the sweep of the storm that the interior of the passage seemed strangely peaceful and still.

The flashlight sliced a brilliant gleam of light from the blackness ahead.

Step by step they advanced across the hard rock. The dampness and cold became more pronounced. As they went on the passage widened and in a few minutes they found themselves in a huge chamber in the earth, a chamber that extended far on into darkness, and they could not see the opposite walls.

A curious rustling sound attracted their attention as soon as they entered the place, and Frank stood still.

"What was that?"

They remained motionless and silent. Away off in the darkness of this subterranean chamber they could hear a scuffling and rustling, and sounds that the boys judged were caused by pattering feet. Frank directed the beam of the flashlight toward them, but the light fell short and they could see nothing.

They advanced several paces. The rustling sounds became multiplied. Then, suddenly, Frank caught sight of two gleaming pinpoints of light glowing from the blackness.

"What's that light?" asked Joe.

"I don't know. I'm going closer."

Frank stepped forward again. As he did so, instead of two pinpoints of light, he saw two more, then two more, until at least a dozen of those strange glowing green spots shone from the darkness, reflected in the glow from the flashlight.

"Animals," he said quietly to Joe.

At the same instant he heard a low, menacing snarl.

The glowing greenish lights began to move rapidly to and fro. Into the radiance of the flashlight shot a lean, grey form that disappeared as swiftly as it came.

A prolonged and wicked snarling rose from the gloom. Frank glanced to one side and saw that two of the greenish lights had moved until they were circling behind him. He leaped back.

"We'd better get out of here!" he said. "Those are wolves."

But when the boys turned to retrace their steps they were confronted by a lean form that barred their way to the cave entrance, and in the glow of the flashlight they saw two greenish eyes that glowed fiendishly and two rows of sharp white teeth bared in defiance.

CHAPTER XX

Down the Shaft

Frank Hardy swung the flashlight, and the wolf before them sprang back, snarling ferociously, into the darkness. The pattering of feet at the back of the huge cavern became more insistent. The boys were conscious of those greenish eyes all about them. The wolves were circling around the cave.

Another wolf joined the animal that barred the entrance. By some animal cunning, they seemed to realize that by so doing they could entrap their prey. The Hardy boys knew that they had wandered into a veritable den of timber wolves who had found in this abandoned mine an ideal refuge and shelter, who had probably made the place their own for years.

The wolves drew closer. The circle was narrowing. The animals were beginning to pace about the cave in long strides, drawing in toward the boys as the circumference of the circle grew smaller.

"Keep the flashlight on," said Joe. "They're afraid of the light."

Frank kept turning slowly about, keeping the glare of the flash full on the circling wolves, and every time its radiance illuminated a gaunt grey form the animal would leap back, snarling, into the shadows.

But as quickly as the light was turned away from one side, the wolves on the other side of the circle would grow bolder and come closer. It was inevitable that in a few minutes the lads would be torn to pieces.

Suddenly Frank thought of the revolver they had seized from Slim Briggs. It was still in his pocket and he had forgotten all about it until this time. With his free hand he reached for the weapon.

Slowly he withdrew it. Then, turning the flashlight directly on one of the snarling beasts, he took aim and fired.

The animal dropped in his tracks with a yelp of pain, and instantly the ranks of the wolves were broken as they fled howling to the darkest corners of the cavern. The stricken wolf writhed and snarled wretchedly for a moment, then lay still.

The boys edged back toward the entrance, but before they could reach it a grey form shot across the circle of light and barred the way with a snarl of defiance. Again they were trapped. Frank fired at the animal. The shot went wide and the brute slunk back, but still remained in the passageway. Two or three of the other animals came rushing out of the darkness and pounced on the body of the dead wolf, tearing at the flesh with savage jaws. For a while the cave echoed with growls and snarls as the animals set about their hideous meal, and then the revolver crashed forth again and another wolf toppled over dead.

"Three shells left," said Frank.

"Save them. We'll take a chance on getting out."

But the chance appeared to be a slim one. More wolves had joined their leader at the entrance, and it seemed impossible that the boys could ever make their escape that way.

The wolves began to advance. The leader came forward, showing his teeth. His eyes glowed like spots of green flame.

Step by step, the boys retreated.

The animals appeared to have overcome their fear of the flashlight. They no longer slunk into the shadows when its fierce glare was turned on them. Instead, they came forward boldly, with dripping, gleaming jaws.

"I'm afraid we're trapped," declared Frank.

"We'll die fighting, anyway. I wish I had a gun."

"Wouldn't be much use against this pack."

"Turn your flash and see if there isn't any other way out of this place except the way we came in."

Frank turned the light swiftly about toward the walls back of them and in the radiant gleam the boys saw a narrow passage, like a dark splotch against the rock, just a few feet away.

"That looks like our only chance."

"We'll try it, anyway. It seems to lead back into the wall quite a distance."

"It may be all right—as long as we don't run into another wolf den."

"Those brutes will follow us."

"The whole pack can't get into that narrow tunnel, at any rate. We'll have a better chance of fighting them off." Frank turned the light swiftly on the dark passage again. "You try it first. They may try to rush us when they see us getting away."

They backed up as close to the opening in the rocks as they could. The wolves were very near now. Three of them had thrust their cruel heads directly into the circle of light from the flash. Their vicious snarling echoed throughout the cave. Frank sensed that they were preparing to spring.

"Quick!" he urged his brother.

Joe leaped and scrambled into the opening.

At the same instant the foremost wolf

crouched for a spring. There was not a second to lose. Frank leveled the revolver and fired.

His aim was true. Halfway in the air the animal gave a convulsive twist of its body and crashed on to the rocks. It writhed in its death agony, snarling ferociously and snapping at everything within reach, until it finally lay still.

The respite was just what the boys needed. The other wolves slunk back, discouraged by the loss of their leader. Frank knew, however, that it would be but for a moment. He backed into the passage with Joe.

The tunnel was narrow, but high enough to permit them to move about without crouching. They were unable to light their way, as Frank needed the flashlight turned before him in order to frighten back the wolves. For a moment the animals seemed to hesitate, as though fearing a trap and then the foremost wolf cautiously entered the tunnel in pursuit of its prey.

The boys backed slowly down the tunnel, which descended on a slope. They did not know where it lead, they could not see, but they knew they must keep backing away from the wolves.

"We're up against it if this is a blind alley," declared Joe, in a low voice.

"We're up against it if we stop and try to fight it out."

Step by step they moved backward, and step by step the foremost wolf pursued them.

The animal was more cowardly than the leader that had been killed. He did not advance boldly, but slunk along, pressing to the side of the tunnel as though trying to evade the dazzling gleam of light that shone in his eyes. Now and then he snarled viciously, showing his teeth.

"Are any of the wolves following him?" asked Joe, from the darkness.

"I can't see any. This brute seems to be alone."

"How about taking a shot at him?"

"What's the use? Even if I did kill him, we'd only run into the rest of them when we went out into the cave again. I'm not going to use this gun again unless I absolutely have to."

The brothers continued their weird journey. The tunnel was damp and chilly. The floor was rocky and uneven, and Frank was in constant dread lest he trip and fall. It would be all up with them then. The wolf would not lose a second in taking advantage of such an opportunity. So, stepping backward, they retreated farther and farther down the passage, watching the grey form that constantly followed, never gaining on them, but never falling back.

"I wonder how long this tunnel is?" Frank muttered.

"Can't last forever," said Joe, with an attempt at cheerfulness. "I think I feel a draft of cold air at my back."

"It doesn't lead outside, that's certain. If it did it would be sloping upward."

There was a low snarl from the wolf. It advanced farther into the circle of light. The brute had evidently decided that the light was not particularly dangerous, and was growing bolder.

Frank tightened his grip on the revolver. The animal was preparing for a rush.

The gaunt grey form gathered itself together and came directly at him.

Frank pressed the trigger.

The revolver crashed forth, awakening thunderous echoes in the narrow tunnel. The wolf gave vent to a howl of pain and fury, but although its onward course was checked for a moment and it swerved to one side it did not fall back. The bullet had not found a vital spot. Maddened by pain, the animal came on again.

The boys scrambled back. The wolf leaped. Frank flung himself to one side and the great body brushed against him. He struck out with the revolver and felt the weapon strike against flesh. Again he pulled the trigger, with the barrel of the weapon directly against the animal's hide, and then he sprang farther back into the tunnel.

Behind him he heard a shout. It seemed curiously far away. He retreated another step.

His foot did not find the solid rock. Instead, he stepped back into space. For an instant he wavered, clutching vainly at the air. Then he lost his balance, staggered backward, and then felt himself falling on downward into utter darkness.

CHAPTER XXI

UNDERGROUND

FRANK HARDY could not have fallen more than ten or twelve feet, but he had the sensation of having dropped from an enormous height. The unexpectedness of it took his breath away, and when he finally crashed into a heap of earth and gravel with a jolt that jarred every bone in his body he could only lie there in the darkness and wonder that he was still alive.

Then, to his relief, came a voice from close at hand.

"Are you all right, Frank?"

"That you, Joe?"

"You didn't expect to find anybody else down here, did you?" asked Joe, with a chuckle.

"I'm all right. No bones broken. How about you?"

"I'm shaken up a bit, but I'm all right Thank goodness I didn't land on my head."

"What on earth happened?"

"We must have stepped right back into the main shaft of the mine. That passage we were in was a drift that went right through to the cave. We're at the bottom of the shaft now, I guess."

Frank had still retained his grasp of the flashlight. Fortunately it had not been broken in the fall and when he switched it on the welcome glow of light again pervaded their prison.

High above them they could see a patch of snow-white sky, sharply outlined by the rectangular shaft-head. A crude ladder ascended the side of the shaft. They could see the black patch that marked the entrance to the drift from which they had fallen, and from it emanated growls and snarls of rage and pain.

"That beast won't follow us any farther. I guess that was why the wolves were so doubtful about chasing us in there. They steer clear of that tunnel," ventured Frank.

"Lucky for us we hit the shaft when we did. That wolf would have been all over us in two more seconds. He'd have made mincemeat out of both of us. I thought sure we were done for, and then I stepped back—wow! I thought I was falling clean through the earth."

"Me, too. I couldn't imagine what had happened. I thought the bottom of the tunnel had given way on us."

"Good thing the shaft isn't any deeper. We'd have saved our lives by escaping from the wolf and broken our necks by falling down the shaft."

"We're lucky. But now we're down here, what are we going to do about it?"

Joe pointed to the ladder.

"We can get to the surface easily enough now."

"But if this is the main shaft we ought to be able to find our way to the blue room mentioned on that map."

"No use backing out now that we've come this far. I'd almost forgotten what we'd come for."

Frank got to his feet. He was not seriously injured by the fall, although he had wrenched one knee. But he was able to walk without much difficulty. He explored the bottom of the shaft with the flashlight. Almost directly across from them he found the entrance to the tunnel indicated on the map he had discovered in the outlaw's notebook.

"Here we are!"

To refresh his memory he drew the notebook from his pocket again and the boys studied the map once more.

"This passage leads to the big chamber, by the looks of it. And when we get there we find two passages leading out of it. We follow this one," Frank indicated the tunnel marked X. "And from there we get to a smaller chamber. We follow a tunnel out of that until we get to what they call the blue room. And there we'll find the gold."

"If the outlaws haven't beaten us to it."

"Perhaps so. But perhaps they haven't."

Frank advanced toward the tunnel, flashing the light before him. It was a large passage and had evidently been frequently used. He examined the damp floor and found footprints that were plainly of recent origin.

"Some one has been here, and not so long ago either."

"To-day?"

"It's hard to tell. Footprints would look fresh down here for weeks, as long as no one else stepped over them. What I mean is that there has been some one down here since the mine was abandoned. That's plain enough."

"Well, it means we're on the right track."

With rapidly growing excitement, the two Hardy boys made their way on into the tunnel. Frank, having the flashlight, took the lead. This tunnel, the main drift of the mine leading into the working level, was not of great length, and within the minute they had reached the first chamber indicated on the map.

In the glow of the flashlight they saw that it was of considerable extent and was bolstered

up by timbers that were now rotting away.
The marks of pickaxes were discernible on the
walls and an overturned wheelbarrow bore
mute testimony to the work that had once gone
on here underground in the search for gold.

Frank turned the light this way and that.
In one corner he found the entrance to a second
corridor leading out of the working, but this
was not the one he wanted. After a few
minutes' search they discovered the tunnel indicated by the cross on the map.

"We're getting warmer," he said, as they
advanced toward it.

The tunnel had heavy timbers at either side,
to support the roof and to prevent a cave-in.
They entered it and stumbled along across the
uneven floor. Water dripped from the ceiling
and from the rocky walls. The dampness and
cold made them shiver.

The tunnel led into a second and smaller
chamber.

"Now for the last passageway. Then to the
blue room!"

They explored the little chamber. But of a
tunnel leading from it there was no sign. A
sloping heap of gravel and boulders lay in one
corner, a broken pickax lay on the floor, and a
rusty shovel stood against the wall. There
were many footmarks on the damp floor, but
there was not the slightest trace of an exit.

"That's funny," murmured Frank, as he turned the beam of the flashlight on the walls. "I'm sure we're in the right place."

He looked at the map again. They had followed the directions exactly, and if the map was correct they should find a tunnel leading from the rocky chamber in which they stood.

"Listen!" said Joe suddenly.

They stood stock-still, not saying a word. The silence of the mine was profound.

"What's the matter?" whispered Frank finally.

"I thought I heard a sound—like some one talking."

They listened again, but they could hear nothing save the occasional drip-drip of water from the walls.

"It must have been my imagination," said Joe, at last. "But I was sure I heard a voice."

"This mine is full of echoes. It was probably only the wind whistling down the shaft."

"I guess that was it. But this place is so creepy a fellow imagines almost anything."

"It would be a tough break for us if the outlaws marched in on us just now."

"I don't think there's much danger. They won't be roaming around in that storm outside."

The boys resumed their search of the cave. They turned the flashlight high and low in the

hope of finding the tunnel that had been so
plainly marked on the plan, but without suc-
cess.

"We must have taken the wrong passage,"
Joe remarked.

"I'm positive we took the right one. I took
special care—But say! Perhaps the tunnel has
been covered up!"

"That's an idea. It may be hidden."

Frank turned the ligh⁺ on the heap of rocks
and gravel in one corner of the cave. At the
base of the pile he could see footprints, all of
which led directly to or from the heap.

"Maybe this is where it is,' he said, and,
handing Joe the flashlight, he picked up the
shovel. He attacked the gravel vigorously,
casting shovelfuls of it to one side. In a few
moments he gave an exclamation of satisfaction. For, back of the gravel he had shoveled
away, he saw a wooden door.

"Now we're getting there!"

The gravel flew, and in a short time the door
was revealed, back of a heap of boulders that
the boys lost no time in rolling to one side. To
their disappointment they found a rusty padlock on the door, but Joe remembered the
broken pickax they had seen in the chamber a
short while before and he seized it. A few
sharp blows and the padlock lay broken and
shattered. He wrenched at the door and it

came slowly open, with a protesting creak of hinges.

Casting the shovel to one side, Frank once more took the lead and they passed through the doorway. The tunnel at this point was very rough and narrow. They made their way cautiously forward. Frank noticed a change in the color of the earth and rock at this juncture.

"It seems blue," he remarked to his brother. Some chemical constituent gave the underground passage that peculiar shade, discernible even in the dim light.

The tunnel narrowed and the boys squeezed their way through the passage, stepping directly into another chamber dug out of the earth. Here the blueness of the walls was intensified, the wet blue earth giving off a weird glow.

"No mistake about it this time!" declared Frank triumphantly. "We're in the blue room at last."

His words echoed and re-echoed in the confined space. The boys were trembling with excitement. The end of their search was at hand. Somewhere in that underground room lay the four bags of gold.

But where?

The floor of the chamber was unbroken. A few faint footprints could be seen, but there was nothing to indicate a secret hiding place. Frank again produced the map.

"Gold at circle," he said, reading from the instructions. "The map shows the circle to be in the far right hand corner." He went forward to the corner indicated. The earth here seemed unusually smooth and flat.

"I think it's buried here," declared Frank. "There's the mark of a shovel."

"I'll get that shovel we had in the other room. Lend me the light for a second."

Frank handed his brother the flashlight, and Joe disappeared from the blue chamber. His footsteps echoed in the narrow passage.

As Frank Hardy waited in the dank darkness, he felt a curious exultation possess him. They were on the verge of solving the mystery of the hidden gold—if only the outlaws had not removed it from its hiding place. He waited in suspense for his brother's return.

CHAPTER XXII

BLACK PEPPER

In a few minutes Frank Hardy saw the gleam of the light and heard his brother's footsteps as Joe returned. He was carrying the shovel that had served them to such good purpose in uncovering the secret door to the passageway of the blue room.

"I'll dig," he volunteered, handing the flashlight to Frank.

Then, with a will, he set to work.

The earth was soft, which showed that it had been dug up before and replaced. Frank held the light, directing its beam on the place where Joe was digging, and as a hole rapidly appeared in the ground he watched eagerly for some sign of the treasure which they sought.

In his mind was always the hated probability that they might have been forestalled and that the outlaws might have already visited the place and removed the gold. But, in that case, he argued to himself, it was not likely that they would have taken such precautions to bank

192

up the locked door of the passage. There would have been no need for it.

"Nothing yet," panted Joe.

"It may be buried deep."

A far-off sound caught Frank's ear. He started violently, because his nerves were already tautened by suspense.

"Did you hear that?" he asked.

Joe rested on the shovel.

"I heard something," he said doubtfully.

They listened, but the sound was not repeated.

"It might have been a fall of rock," said Frank. "It sounded like rocks striking against the walls of the shaft."

"It's just like my thinking I heard voices a while ago. This place is so silent and creepy it gets your nerves all unstrung."

"Maybe."

Joe resumed his shoveling.

Another shovelful of earth and he bent forward.

"Something here!" he exclaimed. "My shovel struck something solid."

Frank brought the flashlight closer. Just above the earth he could see the top of a canvas sack.

"It's the gold! Dig, Joe. Dig!"

Joe Hardy needed no urging. He had seized the shovel again and the earth was flying furiously on all sides. Rapidly, he uncovered the top of the canvas sack, and then a second appeared in view. Frank bent down and seized one of the sacks, dragging it from the retaining earth. It came free. Joe flung aside his shovel and, in the illumination from the flashlight, Frank undid the heavy cord at the top of the sack and opened it.

He thrust his hand inside and withdrew it a moment later, clutching a handful of reddish brown objects that looked like pebbles.

"Nuggets!"

The boys gazed at the gold nuggets in silent delight. They were of good size, and the youths realized that they must be very valuable. Frank thrust his hand into the sack again and this time brought forth a handful of reddish sand that they recognized as gold dust.

"Gold dust and nuggets! We've found it at last!"

"There are more sacks yet. Didn't dad say there were four?"

Joe picked up his shovel again. After a few minutes' energetic digging he uncovered the rest of the sacks and in a short time all four were on the floor of the cave.

The Hardy boys examined each in turn, and found that each was identical with the first in that it contained gold dust and nuggets in large quantities. The sight of so much gold sent a thrill through them, just as it has sent a thrill through gold-seekers since the world began. Here was wealth, wealth in the raw, wealth for which men had fought and struggled, wealth that had been drawn from the depths of the earth.

"We've found it at last!" Frank declared, with a sigh of relief.

"Dad will be pleased."

"I don't think he ever really expected we'd find it."

"We've worked hard enough for it. Won't the outlaws be wild when they come here for it and find that it's gone!"

"Let them be wild. It isn't theirs."

"Four sacks of it," said Joe. "It must be worth thousands."

"It's the gold that Jadbury Wilson mentioned. I'm sure of that. And before we hand it over to Bart Dawson we'll have an explanation from him."

"Somehow, I can't believe he's dishonest. There must be a mistake in it somewhere, Frank."

"You can't always tell by looks in this world. Although, to tell the truth, I find it hard to believe that Dawson made away with this, myself. But we'll make him come across with the whole story, and if he did steal it, we'll see that Wilson gets his share."

"That's the ticket. And now—to get out of this mine with it."

"It'll be easy enough. We can go up the shaft. That's the way the outlaws got in here, I guess. We took the wrong entrance getting in here. We got into one of the side workings of the mine instead of coming down the main way."

"As long as we don't run into any more wolves I don't care how we get out," said Joe. "The sooner we get out though, the better. It must be night by now."

Frank bent and picked up two of the sacks of gold.

"I'll carry two and you carry two. Boy, but they're heavy! I never knew gold weighed so much."

"I shouldn't care if it weighed a ton. It won't seem like much, now that we've found it at last."

Frank hesitated.

"It might be as well to dig a little deeper there. They might have divided the gold up. I'd hate to overlook a sack of it."

"I was just thinking the same thing." Joe picked up the shovel again. "I'll dig down a little bit farther, just for luck."

He attacked the hole in the earth again, and for a while he shoveled industriously, but it soon became apparent that they had found all of the gold that had been buried in that place.

"I guess we got it all," he said, flinging the shovel to one side. "All the outlaws will find here will be a hole in the ground—a big one."

"I'd like to be listening in when they come to look for their treasure. They'll be as mad as hornets."

Joe picked up his two sacks of gold.

"Better let me carry one of yours," he suggested. "You have the flashlight to carry. It'll be awkward for you."

"I'd forgotten about the light," Frank agreed. "All right."

He passed over one of the sacks he had been carrying, and then bent down to pick up the flashlight that had been resting on the ground.

"And now," he said, "we'll leave the blue room. It isn't as blue as Black Pepper and his gang will be when they come to visit the place."

The boys looked at the hole in the ground and chuckled. They were just about to turn, ready to leave, when they heard a sound from the passage leading into the chamber.

This time they knew it was no trick of the imagination. They could sense plainly that some one was standing there. Some one had crept up through the tunnel, unheard, and was even then standing silently in the darkness.

Frank flung the flashlight about. Its circle of radiance illuminated the dark entrance to the chamber clearly. There, in the very center of the opening, stood a tall, swarthy man with villainous features. He had a heavy black beard and his dark eyebrows were knitted with wrath. And, leveled directly at the two boys, he held in each hand a wicked-looking black revolver.

"Hands up!" he rasped curtly, in a voice that vibrated with anger.

The Hardy boys knew without question that this man was none other than the notorious outlaw they had tried to circumvent—Black Pepper!

CHAPTER XXIII

THE CAPTURE

THE Hardy boys were stunned by surprise. With victory in their grasp they had turned to confront this menacing figure that seemed to have risen like a ghost from the darkness. Black Pepper had captured them red-handed.

"Drop that gold!" growled the outlaw. "Drop that gold and put up your hands!"

They faced one another tensely. Suddenly Frank pointed to the tunnel directly behind Black Pepper.

"Grab him!" he shouted.

Almost instinctively, the outlaw wheeled about to face the enemy whom he judged was behind him. Before he realized the trick that had been played on him and while his revolvers were turned away from the two lads, the Hardy boys sprang into action.

Joe flung one of the sacks of gold with all his force. It struck against the outlaw's arm and knocked one of the weapons clattering to the floor. At the same instant Frank flung the sack that he was carrying, and it struck Black Pepper in the chest.

The outlaw reeled backward. The Hardy boys leaped toward him.

Frank was on him before he could raise his remaining weapon. Like a flash, he seized Black Pepper's arm, holding the revolver away from him. Then Joe joined the struggle and between the two of them they bore the outlaw to the ground by the sheer violence of their attack.

Grimly, Black Pepper struggled. The flashlight had gone out, and the battle raged in complete darkness. It was difficult to tell friend from foe. The outlaw was strong and powerful and he wrestled desperately to get free.

Frank clung grimly to the outlaw's arm, exerting all his strength to prevent Black Pepper from getting control of the revolver. The weapon exploded in the darkness, the shot sounding like a crash of thunder in that confined space.

Frank got his hands on the revolver and wrested sharply at it. Black Pepper's grasp relaxed. The revolver gave way and Frank wrenched it away from the outlaw. Quickly he reversed it and pressed the barrel against Black Pepper's body.

"Put up our hands!" he snapped. "I have you covered."

Black Pepper ceased his struggles and lay still.

"I give in," he said quickly. "I give in. Don't shoot."

"Get the flashlight, Joe."

Joe relinquished his grasp on the outlaw and searched for the flashlight, which had rolled to a distant corner of the cave. He found it at last and switched it on. The light revealed Black Pepper lying on his back, his hands upraised. His eyes were wide with fear.

"Get up!" ordered Frank.

The outlaw scrambled to his feet, arms still high.

"Get the other gun, Joe."

Joe found the other revolver on the floor and picked it up.

"Fine! Now we'll take you back with us."

"Let me go, boys," pleaded the desperado. "It was only a joke. I was only tryin' to scare you. Take the gold, if you want, but let me go."

"You have a funny idea of a joke. Well, just as a joke, we'll take you down to Lucky Bottom and clap you into jail. That's the kind of a sense of humor we have. Pick up the gold, Joe, and go ahead of him. I'll come behind."

Armed with the flashlight and two sacks of gold, Joe went to the entrance of the blue room. Frank picked up the other two sacks and, still keeping Black Pepper covered with a revolver, urged him ahead.

"Forward, march!" he ordered.

Reluctantly, the outlaw strode ahead, following Joe, who was silhouetted against the circle of light cast by the flash.

"My men will see that you pay up for this!" he growled savagely.

"Your men will be scattered so far you'll never be able to find them when they hear you've been taken in," replied Frank. "If they don't, they'll land in jail with you. How did you happen to be down in the mine without them? Trying to make away with the gold in the storm?"

The shot told. Black Pepper looked around sharply.

"I wasn't trying to double-cross them!" he shouted. "Don't tell them that! Don't say you found me down here. None of us was supposed to go in here alone."

Frank chuckled.

"So that was your game, was it? You thought you'd sneak down here and grab the gold, then make your escape under cover of the blizzard. If we hadn't got here first, you would have done it, too. Your men will be liable to take revenge on us after that, won't they? Why, they'll want to see you hanged!"

Black Pepper was silent. His bluff had

failed, and he knew it. He knew that when the
other outlaws heard he had been captured in
the blue room they would realize that he had
been trying to steal a march on them and make
away with the gold without their knowledge.

Joe led the way down the passage into the
next chamber, and from there they proceeded
out into the main shaft.

"I guess we were right after all when he
thought we heard noises," he called back to
Frank. "It was our friend here making his
way down into the mine."

"He came down quietly enough. I nearly
jumped out of my shoes when I saw him standing there with those revolvers pointed at us.
We'll say that much for you, Black Pepper—
you took us completely by surprise."

The outlaw grunted, but it was not with satisfaction.

Joe began to ascend the ladder that led up
the side of the shaft.

"Up you go," declared Frank, prodding the
desperado in the ribs with the barrel of the
revolver. Black Pepper scrambled up the rungs
with alacrity.

They made the tedious climb without trouble,
and when Joe emerged at the top of the shaft
he took up his position and covered Black
Pepper with the revolver until the outlaw was
again on the surface and until Frank had joined

him. The blizzard had died down to a mild snowfall, although darkness had fallen.

Far below, they could see the few twinkling lights of Lucky Bottom. A clearly defined trail led out toward the road. Joe took the lead once more.

So the odd procession made its way through the snow, the outlaw shambling despondently and dispiritedly between his captors. The weight of the gold was considerable, but Frank and Joe scarcely noticed it, so exultant were they over their double victory. They had not only recovered the gold for its rightful owners, but they had captured one of the most notorious outlaws of the West in the bargain.

When they reached Hank Shale's cabin they marched Black Pepper up to the door. Joe stepped inside and, still covering the outlaw, bade him enter.

Frank saw his father sitting up in bed, wide-eyed with astonishment, and Hank Shale and Bart Dawson by the fire, their mouths agape. Bart Dawson had just been in the act of putting his pipe in his mouth as they entered, and he held it suspended, staring at the trio as they came into the cabin.

Joe flung down his sacks of gold on the table.

"Here's the gold—part of it, anyway!"

"And here's the rest of it," said Frank as he closed the door and put down his two sacks.

"And here," he said, indicating Black Pepper, "is the leader of the gang who stole it."

"Black Pepper!" ejaculated Hank Shale, starting up.

The outlaw was silent. He eyed Frank's revolver warily, as though even yet considering his chances of escape. But the weapon did not waver and he saw that he was trapped.

"Got a rope?" asked Frank of Hank Shale. "He must be tired keeping his hands up. We'll tie his wrists and then march him down to the jail."

"I'll say I have a rope!" shouted Hank, springing up, and within a few minutes Black Pepper's arms were firmly bound behind his back.

"But where on airth did ye find the gold?" demanded Bart Dawson, spluttering with excitement. "Tell us what happened! It's the very gold that was stolen!" He dug his hands into the sacks and sifted the gold dust and nuggets between his fingers. "It's all here— every bit of it! Tell us all about it, lads."

"Take him down to jail first," said Fenton Hardy quietly. "I'm as curious as any one to hear what happened, but the boys can tell us when they come back. The story will keep. But don't be long."

"I'll go with ye!" declared Dawson, picking up his hat and scrambling into his mackinaw coat. "This is too good to miss. I never thought I'd see the day when Black Pepper would be shoved into the calaboose!"

So, with Bart Dawson chattering excitedly by their sides, the Hardy boys left the cabin, where Fenton Hardy and Hank Shale were indulging in vain conjectures as to how the gold had been recovered and how the outlaw had been captured.

As they entered Lucky Bottom, although it was nightfall and people had long since retired indoors, the news quickly spread, by some mysterious system of telegraphy or mental telepathy, and by the time they reached the jail, husky miners and citizens were running down the street from every direction, anxious to witness the spectacle of Black Pepper being put behind the bars at last.

The sheriff was in his office and his jaw sagged with amazement when they entered.

"Here's Black Pepper for ye!" roared Bart Dawson. "Here's a prisoner for your jail, sheriff! Clap him in a good strong cell!"

"B—B—Black Pepper!" stammered the sheriff.

"This is him. And see that he don't get loose, neither. If he does, we'll string you up to a telygrapht pole."

"What's the charge?" asked the sheriff mechanically.

"There don't need to be no charge. You know as well as I do that there's been a reward of five hundred out for Black Pepper for the last three years. Put him in a cell, and no more of your foolish questions. If you must have a charge, put him down for stealin' four bags of gold that never belonged to him. Charge him with vagrancy and loiterin' and spittin' on the sidewalk. Charge him with mayhem and assault and battery and horse-stealin' and robbery and carryin' concealed weapons and parkin' his autymobile too close to a hydrant. Put him down for everythin' you've got on your book. He's been guilty of 'em all."

The sheriff wilted. He led Black Pepper to a cell, where Slim Briggs was sitting despondently. When Slim saw the leader of the gang being ushered in he shook his head in sympathy and groaned.

The door clanged.

"That fixes Black Pepper!" declared Bart Dawson, with satisfaction. "Now come on back to the cabin and tell us all about it. I'm just about dyin' of curiosity."

Dawson and the Hardy boys left the jail and had to fight their way through the crowd that surged about the doorway. Questions were hurled at them as they started up the street. Was it true that Black Pepper had been captured at last? Who caught him? What was he in for? How did it all happen, anyway?

"Tell ye all to-morrow," promised Bart Dawson, leading the boys on up the hill. "I'm not very clear about it just yet, myself."

So the Hardy boys returned to Hank Shale's cabin on the hill, there to tell the tale of their hazardous adventures and the successful outcome of their search for the hidden gold.

CHAPTER XXIV

Bart Dawson Explains

Sitting beside the fire in Hank Shale's cabin, the Hardy boys told their story. They were interrupted frequently by ejaculations of "Ye don't say!" and, "Well I'll be switched!" from the two old miners, and occasionally their father smiled in approval.

When they had finished, Bart Dawson slapped his knee.

"I never heard the beat of it!" he declared. "Ye went up on that there mountain and got lost and attacked by wolves and fell down the shaft and got held up by Black Pepper, and yet here ye are, and there's the gold. I never heard the beat!"

"Neither did I!" affirmed Hank Shale slowly.

"There's the gold," laughed Frank, indicating the four sacks on the table.

"Coulson will be tickled to death," declared Bart Dawson. "He never expected either of us to see it again."

"There's a question we wanted to ask you,"

put in Frank. "Are you sure there isn't any-body else but Mr. Coulson sharing the gold with you?"

Fenton Hardy looked up startled. He could not imagine what this was leading to. As for Bart Dawson, he looked blank.

"Not that I know of," he said.

"Are you quite sure?"

"I'm certain sure. There's Coulson's brother did own a share of it, but he's dead, and there's Jadbury Wilson, my old pardner, but he's dead, too. That leaves only me and Coulson."

"Are you sure Wilson is dead?"

"Last we heard of him he was. He went East, they say, and died out there. I sure wish he could be here to-night. Poor old Jad—he worked so hard for his share of that gold, and never got none of it."

"Jadbury Wilson isn't dead."

"What?" shouted Bart Dawson, leaping to his feet. "Say them words again, lad! Do ye know for sure? Is Jad Wilson still livin'?"

"He's staying at our house in Bayport right now," declared Joe.

Fenton Hardy looked more surprised than ever. The case was taking an angle he had never anticipated.

"If I'm sure Jad Wilson is still alive I'll be the happiest man in the world!" declared Bart

Dawson. "But how do ye know? Tell me about him."

The Hardy boys thereupon told of their meeting with Jadbury Wilson and of the story he had told of his gold-mining days in the West.

"So he thinks that you stole the gold from him and went away with it," concluded Frank.

"I don't blame him for thinkin' that!" said Dawson heartily. "I don't blame him a bit! When I come back to Lucky Bottom I made it my business to trace up my old pardners, but the only one I could find was Coulson, and he told me his brother and Jad Wilson was dead."

"But what had happened to the gold?"

"I'm comin' to that. When the outlaws attacked our camp, the others sent me out to hide the gold. And I hid it. I was just gettin' away when a stray bullet hit me, and I'll be hanged if I didn't go clean off my head. I didn't remember nothin'. I must have wandered away from Lucky Bottom altogether, for when I come to myself I was miles and miles away, up in northern Montana, and I couldn't remember one thing of my life up to that time. It had been wiped clean out of my memory. I had papers on me that had my name written on them, but I didn't know where I had come from or nothin'."

"I have heard of such cases," said Fenton Hardy.

"I had clean lost my memory. I didn't even know I had ever been in Lucky Bottom. Everythin' was blank up to the time I come to myself. Then, a few months ago, a doctor told me he thought he could fix me up, and I had an operation and—click! I remembered everythin'. I remembered Lucky Bottom and our mine, and how I had hidden the gold. It all come back to me. So I came back to Lucky Bottom and dug up the gold again and tried to find my pardners, and Coulson and I was ready to split it up between us, seein' we thought his brother and Jad Wilson was dead, when the outlaws stole it on us. So that's how it happened."

Frank and Joe had listened entranced.

"Why, that explains everything!" Frank declared. "It clears it all up. We couldn't believe you had been crooked, although—" he stopped in confusion.

"Although it looked mighty like it, eh?" finished Bart Dawson, with a smile. "Well, I don't blame ye for bein' suspicious. And now, if you'll take me back East with ye, I'll meet my old pardner, Jad Wilson, again, and he'll get his share of the gold. It should be enough to keep him in comfort for all the rest of his life."

"He's been having a pretty tough time," said Frank. "He'll welcome it."

"And glad I'll be to see that he gets his share. As for you, Mr. Hardy," went on Dawson, turning to the detective. "I promised you a good fee if ye'd take this case for me and I promised you a reward if the gold was found. Two thousand dollars, I said, and two thousand dollars you'll get as soon as I can get these nuggets and the gold dust changed into real money."

"I won't take it all," said Fenton Hardy. "My boys did the real work."

"That's up to you. It was your case and you can do what you like with the money. But," Dawson declared with emphasis, "if ye don't divvy up with these two lads——!"

"Don't worry," laughed the detective. "I have no intention of letting them work for nothing. I want to share the reward with them."

"Well, that's fine, then. And they get five hundred dollars for capturin' Black Pepper— don't forget that." Bart Dawson turned to the Hardy boys. "Ye ought to have a nice fat bank account when you go back East."

"It begins to look that way," agreed Frank, with a pleased smile.

"You've done good work," said Fenton Hardy. "You've cleaned up this case in record time and, to tell the truth, I hardly expected you would be successful, because you were up against a mighty difficult undertaking and you didn't have very much to work on. You deserve everything that is coming to you in the way of reward. You've done me credit.''

Before very long these boys were to bring honor again to the Hardy name. In solving "The Shore Road Mystery" they were going to need every ounce of energy and intelligence with which Nature had endowed them.

"I'm very proud of you," said Mr. Hardy.

"Hearing you say that is reward enough," said Frank, and Joe nodded his head in agreement.

"Real detectives, both of 'em," said Hank Shale, puffing at his pipe.

THE END